Nearly all of us are guilty of wasting the precious days of our lives.

Do not be consumed with the dollar; it will keep you awake at night.

Stop and think, what do we need other than Love, Good Health, Food, and Shelter.

Take time to enjoy this beautiful earth while you are still on the green side of the turf.

Chapter 1

No Time to Lose

Farron's strong weathered face broke quickly into a smile as the crew from another fishing vessel asked about today's catch. Eyes, as blue as the sea, snapped with excitement, "Ask the crew," he replied and turned to the men sitting in the corner booth. "The Tuna tried to eat the boat; we nearly busted our asses, pulling them in. Every boat was loaded; we had to wait in line at the cannery to unload."

"I don't know about busting your ass, honey," a soft little voice said, as a hand caressed his bottom, "feels to me like both cheeks are there."

Farron put his hand over the tiny hand on his behind, turned, bent down, and kissed Mary on the lips, "You sweet little thing, why didn't you wait for me on the pier?"

"Because I knew you would be here; must I remind you that you have a date with some important people. You've got to rest, clean up, and look like a movie star."

A roar came from the corner booth as the men held their glasses up and shouted, "We'll drink to that! Be sure to take a picture!"

"You see what you started! I'll never hear the last of this! Why don't you send my regrets; tell them I'm still out fishing?"

"No, Farron; your dad wants you to do this."

Farron downed his drink and waved to the crew, "See you in a couple of days, guys, got to take this sweet thing home."

"Be sure she washes your back," they chimed and laughed.

Farron put a big hand on Mary's shoulder, "Oh, she will," he replied, "you should all be so lucky!"

Born Scotch-Irish, Farron's father, Blaine McClaine, a large big-hearted man, loved poetry, music, fishing, and his fragile little wife, a dark-eyed Irish beauty, Cecile Toner. Blaine owned and ran a grain elevator in South Bend, Indiana, made a comfortable living, and lived without worry until Cecile's asthmatic condition worsened. After the birth of their son, following doctor's advice, Blaine sold their home and bought a boarding house on the beach in Long Beach, California, away from Indiana humidity. There, Cecile had less trouble breathing. Farron grew, ran the beaches, loved the sea, and became a commercial fisherman. Now, he was a man happy with life and interested in only two things; Mary and fishing the ocean.

As Mary straightened his tie, Farron grumbled, "Honey, I see no point in this, and pulled off the tie. We do not belong to the Hollywood crowd. Why get involved in something about which we know nothing? We have a pleasant life, and I'm happy with things the way they are. Is there something more you want that I can't give?"

"Of course not; all I need in life is you, but Farron, you should do this to please your father. You know how he is about the theatre; he's a ham actor and gets every part he can in the local 'Little Theatre.'"

Grumbling, Farron continued, "Yeah, yeah, he's the one who should go. Come here and let me explain something to you."

Mary sat on the edge of the bed, while Farron pulled a chair up in front of her and took both her small hands in his. "Honey, I believe in past lives and feel I've lived more than one. Have you ever been someplace and felt as if you'd been there before. When we met, we were not strangers; we belonged together."

"That's true," Mary agreed, and stretched out on the bed, "Come, lie beside me; I want to feel your arms around me."

Farron pulled off his shirt and stretched alongside Mary, "This is better than going to a shindig with a bunch of Swells? If dad asks what happened, I'll tell the truth; I fished all day and was too tired to go. Mary, when I'm at the helm, I look up at the stars, and I am one with God. There is nothing like being on the sea, with no sound other than that of my ship cutting through the water. Now and then, a horn will blow as another ship warns of nearness, and below, the men stretch out on bunks and snore. As if calling me, an unseen hand guides me to the fish. I was born for the sea, and you; we must have loved in another life."

Mary ran her hand across his chest and kissed him, "I love you so much it's easy to give into you, but not this time, Farron.

I think you should shower and go to that party, or whatever it is. You should do this for Blaine; he is so proud of you. And I think you should, at least, learn what they are offering. It might be something worthwhile."

Farron breathed a heavy sigh, "Will you go with me?"

"They did not invite me, Farron, they invited you. I'll keep the bed warm for you," she giggled.

"It's warm enough right now," he answered, pulled her to him, and in a while, out of breath, headed for the shower. "I'm doing this for you, Mary, not for dad."

Mary got out of bed and followed him into the shower, "Don't forget, I have to wash you back." She quickly showered, got out, and said, "I'll have your Martini waiting."

A few minutes later, Farron entered the living room wearing a lightweight summer suit, "I hope this will do for the upper-crust."

"You will be the best looking man there," she replied as she eyed him from head to toe, "they may think a fisherman doesn't know how to dress; well, they are in for a surprise. That ascot makes you look like a rich playboy. I love you. Now, give your dad a call and let him know you are not going to disappoint him."

At a glance, the soiree, held at a large mansion in Beverly Hills, took Farron's breath away. An attendant held his car door open, directed him to the house, and parked his car, and as he entered, one of the men who had approached him on the pier

came to him and shook his hand, "In case you've forgotten, I'm Sol; we were afraid you might not join us, had you not, we would have come to you. Have a drink, and I'll explain." A waiter came with a tray of wine, Farron took a glass, and Sol continued. "I know you are puzzled and questioning our interest in you. It's like this, Morty, and I have a little project, a movie we've put together and presented to the studios; they accepted the idea, and, now, we are anxious to get it off the ground. We have an interesting script that calls for an expert fisherman, one with knowledge of the sea. When we spotted you on the pier, mending nets, we agreed that you were the perfect person, big, weathered, handsome, and a fisherman."

Morty saw them coming, excused himself from the others, and held out his hand to Farron. "I'm so glad you came; I suppose you worked today and don't relish being here with us, so we will not detain you long." He nodded to Sol,

"Let's go out on the balcony away from all this noise and tell Farron what we have in mind."

Farron had not yet said a word, other than good-evening. He laughed, "That will be much appreciated. I am puzzled and out of my element; I am a fisherman, and this is a first for me. When I drive by mansions such as this, I look and wonder why anyone would care to live in a house with so many rooms."

Both men laughed, and Sol said, "My wife forced me into this; women like to entertain."

The air was fresh, with a soft westerly breeze; they sat at a

round table, the waiter-served drinks and hors d'oeuves, and Mort began to explain. "Mister McClaine, I suppose Sol told you that we are planning to make a movie about a commercial fisherman who fishes the Bering Straits near Nome, Alaska. We have a story, a leading lady, a crew of men, and a ship; what we don't have is a male lead. Of course, we are not shy of actors who would love this part, but we need a real fisher. When we saw you, we thought, if this man can act, he is perfect for the part."

Farron began to laugh, "Excuse me, gentlemen, I'm afraid you have chosen the wrong person. Needless to say, I am complimented; however, I have no desire to be an actor. I have a home, a beautiful wife, a ship, a crew, and the sea. I have everything a man could want. Today we brought in tons of Tuna and left it at the cannery to be canned, labeled, and sold in the markets. I am tired, and to be perfectly honest, I should be home in bed; it has been a very long day."

Mort persuasively continued, "It is presumptuous of me to ask how much money you earn per year, but at a guess, I would say around thirty-six thousand, am I right?"

Farron grinned and evasively replied, "Well, it depends on the year and the fish."

Mort continued, "Well, McClaine, how would you like to earn three-hundred-fifty thousand for three weeks in Alaska?"

Farron tossed his drink back, coughed, and looked from one man to the other. "Are you serious? Is this some kind of a gag?"

Sol spoke up, "We are not joking. We know you are not an actor, but you have the looks; you are a professional captain and fisherman. We need someone who knows the sea, someone who can handle a boat in any kind of weather, someone who would not panic in a storm on high seas. As for the acting, you would be doing what comes naturally; the script is minor."

Puzzled, Farron asked, "What kind of a story is it? You said you have a leading lady; where does she fit into the script? How many women in the cast? Is it one of those films about bars and dancing girls, or is it about men, the sea, and fishing."

Sol replied, "It is difficult to make a film without a woman in it; the public expects to see a leading lady. This picture, for the most part, is about fishing, and a woman who loves a man, and fears she will lose him to the sea."

Farron began to shake his head, "No. I'm sorry; the money is enticing, but I cannot make love to a woman in a film. I am a married man; I love my wife more than I love money. You need to find a different man. Look at some of the other men in my crew; there are some big good looking men on my boat who would jump at the chance to make a movie."

"Not so fast," Mort answered, "you said you have a wife, and you love her more than money; why don't you run this by her; you might find that she would love to have you make our film. If you wish, you can take her with you."

Again, Farron laughed, "Here's what I'll do; when I get home

I will tell Mary all about your proposition, and if she thinks I should do it, we can all have lunch on the pier and talk it over. The one thing that interests me is the idea of going to Alaska. I would love to fish the Bering Straits."

"It was difficult," Mort continued, "to engage a commercial fishing boat and crew, but we did. Of course, for the filming, you are the captain of the ship. The companies regular captain will be at the helm most of the time. Also, another ship will follow yours for long-distance shots."

The excitement of going to Alaska and fishing the Bering Straits began to race through Farron's veins. His face flushed, his blue eyes sparkled with excitement, and Sol and Mort knew they had hooked him. "I can hardly wait to tell Mary and my dad about your offer. It's like a dream come true, but if my Mary doesn't like the idea, I won't do it. My marriage is worth more than my dreams."

"Okay," Mort said, "run it by your wife and father, and we can meet again in a day or so. You pick the place, and we will be there." He handed Farron his business card and continued, "I believe you already have one of these, but just in case, here's another. Call me when you are ready."

Two days later, Farron, Mary, Blaine, Mort, and Sol sat at a table on the pier. Mort explained everything to Blaine and Mary and spread a contract out on the table in front of Farron. All three looked it over before Farron would sign. He nervously looked at Mary and said, "Now honey, if you don't want me to do this, just say the word. I know it's a lot of money, but we have everything we need, and if you are afraid for me to be away for so long, I won't do it."

Blaine interrupted, "Listen, son, this is a once in a lifetime offer; if I were your age, I would take it. You don't need to worry about Mary; Cecile and I will see that she is taken care of."

Mary's hands shook as she held Farron's, "I know you are aching to go to Alaska, it has been your dream for years, and I will do nothing to stand in your way. As you have said, it's not for the money; it is to fulfill a dream."

All agreed, Farron signed the contract and three weeks later was on his way to Alaska.

Chapter 2

At the airport, fighting against showing she was ill, Mary kissed Farron and told him to enjoy the fishing. "I wish you were going with me," he replied, "I will miss my little Mary. As soon as I'm settled and have a phone number, I will call you and tell you all about Alaska, and I'll take pictures and send them." He pulled her into his arms and kissed her. "Take care of yourself, Mary, it won't be long; three months will go by quickly."

The plane lifted off the ground, and Mary ran for a bathroom; she had morning sickness, and kept it her secret because she knew had Farron known, he would not have gone. Blaine saw her pause, put her hand on her head, and move on. He tried to rush to her side; she looked as if she were going to pass out, but before he could reach her, she vanished behind closed doors. Waiting, and worried, he was about to send someone in when Mary appeared, looking pale as a ghost. Blaine rushed to her side, "Are you alright?"

Mary leaned against Blaine, "I am now, but I was so afraid this would happen before Farron got on the plane. I am pregnant and didn't want him to know. He will only be away for three months, and when he returns, I'll be big and surprise him."

"You surely will!" Blaine exclaimed. "How long have you know that you are with child?"

"Two months," Mary replied, "and when he gets off the plane, he will find a fat little wife." She laughed.

"Cecile and I will look after you while Farron's away, and she will be so happy with this news. You must come and stay with us until Farron returns."

"I would love to do that, but how will I explain it to Farron?"

Blaine laughed, "Farron and I talked before he left, and he asked me to try and persuade you to stay with us, so he will be pleased. Now let's get your things and move you into Farron's old room; you will be comfortable there."

Cecile greeted Mary with open arms, and Blaine said, "Take this expectant mother up to Farron's room; she needs a rest."

Cecile backed away and eyed Mary, "You are expecting? Does Farron know?"

"No, mom; I didn't tell him because if I had, he would not have gone."

Cecile agreed, "Follow me, and we'll get you comfortable; you look as if you could use a rest and a bite to eat."

"Rest is the answer, and food later," Mary answered, and looked around the room at the pictures on the wall and dresser. "These pictures of Farron make me feel like he is here. I can't thank you enough for having me." She sat on the edge of the bed, kicked off her shoes, and lay back, "This feels wonderful." She closed her eyes and wondered where Farron was, if he was thinking of her, or if his mind was on Alaska.

Farron was not thinking of Mary; seated in first-class, with

a glass of wine in hand, he listened as Mort explained the script. As you can see, the first part of the film takes place in a saloon. There's not much going on at this point; it's just a way to introduce you to the public. Nome's Board of Trade Saloon is a fun place, filled with fishermen and ladies, serves beer and liquor, has a pool room and a jukebox. We have suites at the beautiful Seascape Inn, with a view of the sea and surrounding mountains covered with snow. You will think you are on vacation; the real work starts on board ship, a fifty-eight-foot commercial purse seiner, complete with crew and captain.

Farron interrupted, "A Captain; I thought I was the captain!"

"Yes, of course, you will be filmed at the helm; however, because you do not know these waters, for insurance purposes, we must use the ship's registered captain and crew. They are all thrilled because they are doing their jobs and earning extra money as actors. There will be cameras and cameramen on board, and following your ship, another boat carrying camera operators and cameras for long shots of the ship at sea."

Farron shook his head and looked downhearted; this adventure was not at all what he expected. If possible, he would tear up the contract and head for home. But, of course, he knew he could not, and he would see this thing through no matter how disappointing.

As the plane lowered to come in for a landing, Farron looked out the window and could not escape the thrill of seeing snow-capped mountains. Perhaps one day he would return with Mary, and they would fish the rivers and lakes. A cabin in the hills, and Mary beside him, would be heaven.

Sol smiled at Farron, "I will be here long enough to see you settled, and then, I will return to California; Mort will remain to assure all goes well."

Speechless, Farron nodded and tried to foresee the future. The plane landed, taxied around the field, and stopped.

As Farron's feet touched the ground, he shivered and laughed, "I hope Mary packed my long underwear!"

They went directly to the Seascape Inn, and each had individual suites complete with everything but long-distance phone service. Disappointed, Farron made himself comfortable and resolved to write Mary that night, but when would it reach her? The desk clerk told him it would take a week. He looked around and saw Mort and Sol seated at a table in the dining room and joined them. "This is nice," he declared, "I didn't expect accommodations like this in Nome."

Sol laughed, "Yes, almost makes me want to stay, but I'll be gone the first thing in the morning."

"I hate to see you leave, but Farron and I will be busy." Mort said, "I'd like to have the players meet here in the conference room, but chose the Board of Trade Saloon. It's a fun place with a bar, pool tables, music, fish and chips, and crews from all the ships. Farron will meet his crew, the Captain, and his leading lady; she chose to be alone and is staying at the Aurora Inn."

Nervously, Farron toyed with his napkin, "I think I need a drink; this is all a little much for me. I had hoped to be in touch with my wife, Mary, but can't call from here."

"Since I leave in the morning, Farron," Sol offered, "write a linc to her, and I'll deliver it."

"Wonderful, thank you! I took a few pictures on my cell phone and will add a message." Farron handed Sol the phone, "Take a picture of me to add and give the phone to my wife; it will make her happy."

"Walk outside with me, Farron; I'll take several pictures of you, the Inn, and the Sea, and she'll feel as if she's here. As the plane circled the harbor, I looked out the window and took a few pictures. I also have a folder to give to her with pictures of the ships in the harbor. The folder has stories in it about the ships, the fishing, and the fishermen. Perhaps, all this will encourage her to come and be with you."

"That's very kind of you, Sol, but I think Mary is better off staying with my mother and father. Farron laughed, "When she hears about the leading lady, she might get jealous. I suppose there will be pictures of us in the news?"

All three men laughed, and Mort said, "You have yet to meet her, and you could be right because your co-star, Belle Fauche', is a French, petite, raven-haired beauty. I know she would make my wife insanely jealous."

The following day, shortly after Sol left, Mort and Farron

entered the Board of Trade Saloon, a group of men at the bar lifted their glasses and greeted Mort. One tall, handsome man wearing a Captain's hat approached them, held out his hand, and said, "Greetings mate, I and the crew are anxious to hear all about this venture." He looked at Farron and continued, "This must be our captain from the U.S."

Mort quickly introduced Farron to Captain Bill Armstrong, "Yes, Captain meet

Captain, Farron McClaine." He turned to Farron, "and Farron meet captain Bill Armstrong."

Farron gripped Bill's hand, noting how much he reminded him of his father; strong, sturdy, thick white eyebrows, and deep blue piercing eyes; for a moment, he groped for words, and finally exclaimed, "I am pleased to make your acquaintance. I understand that you will be at the helm most of the time, but let me assure you; I am a competent helmsman. I am a commercial fisherman, have a boat and crew, fish the San Clemente Islands for Bluefin Tuna, and the Channel Islands for Yellowtail. We had a record catch of Tuna to drop off at the cannery before we left to come here."

Bill smiled; he liked this young fellow who obviously enjoyed his work, so why this acting thing? No doubt, as with himself, they made him an offer he couldn't refuse. "I think we'll get along just fine, Farron, come, have a beer with the men and me. The crew, and the two fellows with their cameras, will make us ten aboard ship. I hope those cameramen have sea legs," he laughed.

Six men standing at the bar nodded as the Captain neared, and each reached for Farron's hand as he said their names; Sam, Willie, Frank,

Heinie, John, and Bernie. "This young man, Farron, will be with us on our next trip; he is also a helmsman and Tuna fisherman, has a boat and crew in California and knows the sea. Get your drinks and join us at that round table in the corner.

All grabbed their drinks and started to follow but stopped as a lady they had never seen entered.

Mort grinned, "Gentlemen, we are making a movie, and I want you all to meet our leading lady, Belle Fauche'. She will not be on the ship at any time; however, she will be here, as will the cameramen, and lights, so get used to seeing her."

"Aye," one of the men exclaimed, "that's easy enough!" All laughed, as did Farron until she came to him, took his hand, and said, "I've been anxious to meet you. We don't have much of a script, but we do need to go over it together before we start filming. Perhaps, Mort can arrange a time and place for us to meet."

Farron stood up and held a chair for her, "I am not an actor; you will need patience."

Belle leaned against him, looked up into his eyes, and, with a French accent, replied, "I will teach you."

From somewhere in the room, a camera flashed.

"Join us," Mort agreed, "get acquainted, and tomorrow, we will meet in the conference room at the Seascape Inn."

Belle turned to Captain Armstrong, "Will this handsome man be joining us?"

Eyes flashing, Captain Bill smiled down at her, "My bad luck," he replied, "I am not your co-star; I am one of the crew."

"Quel dommage!" Belle replied.

"Mon malheur, je n'ai pas le temps," Captain Bill, replied.

"Peut-etre Plus tard?" Belle coquettishly answered.

The Captain smiled, "Avec de la chance!"

Farron looked at Mort, "Do you know what they are saying?"

The men at the table laughed, and Mort replied, "A little flirtation; not part of the movie!"

Late the next day, Belle arrived for the conference with Farron and Mort, and Mort was angry. "Belle, when I say morning, I do not mean afternoon. In the future, be on time, or I will cut your part out of the film. Do not think you are indispensable; your part is small, and you can be replaced!"

"I am so sorry," Belle begged, "I will not let it happen again; I overslept, I stayed up going over the script." She turned to Farron, "Have you looked at the script?"

Farron nodded, "It looks as if we are supposed to be in the throes of a romance, but you have another man, one of the crewmen; a fight in the pub, you try to stop it, and in doing so, you get hurt. There follows a pathetic love scene in which I say I'm sorry, and you beg me to give up fishing. Then follows more words with me telling you how and why I can never give up the sea and so forth and so on.

Looking surprised, Belle backed away and said, "Ma Cherie, you are quick, and you are very handsome! You must have studied your script!"

Farron frowned, and in an anxious tone of voice, warned, "Belle, you are a beautiful lady, and you enjoy teasing men; I saw that last night with you and Captain Bill, but do not try that with me. If we are to get along while making this movie, you must understand this; I have a beautiful wife, and I love her. I do not need or want another woman. So please save all your charm for the movie."

Enraged, Belle spat back at Farron, "Comment oses-tu me, parler comme ca. Tu n'es rien!" Red-faced and shaking, she turned to Mort, "You tell this nobody, that I am an actress, and I have no personal interest in him. He has a high opinion of himself, this Ameri-can!"

Mort got out of his chair and looked at both, "Alright! I've had enough of this! "Belle, you are used to having men fall all over themselves to get to you. Now, for the first time, you've met a man you cannot arouse, and you are angry, but you must eat that anger if you want to go to the United States. You accepted this film to open a door for you in Hollywood, so eat your pride. You had success with Captain Bill, isn't that enough?"

Surprised, Farron exclaimed, "What?"

As if he had not heard Farron, Mort continued, "Farron is not an actor and makes no pretense; he accepted this part for one reason only, to fish the Bering Straits, and was disappointed to hear he would have a female co-star. The only thing he can lose by walking out, quitting this film is money because he would have to buy off his contract." Taking a deep breath, Mort sat down, "Now, I want to see you two get to work. I don't care how much you hate each other; show me some action, because tomorrow we start shooting in the saloon, and when finished there, we board the ship and go to sea for a few days or weeks. I don't know how long; it will depend on the weather and the fish."

"I'm willing," Farron said and followed it with an apology to Belle. "Belle, I did not mean to insult you. Mort is right; if we are going to make a movie, let's do it."

She smiled, and they began.

Chapter 3

Fishermen crowded around the bar and filled the tables as the action began. Belle, dressed in a Peasant skirt and revealing lowcut blouse, neared Farron, touched his face with one of her hands, kissed him, and flirting, went from one man to another.

In a throaty voice, Belle began to sing: Look at me; I am Mademoiselle de Paris. Oh, la la, light of heart and fancy-free, I'm the spirit of Spring in gay Paris. When I stroll down the Rue de la Paix on a beautiful day in May, men turn to look at me, the Mademoiselle de Paris.

Belle continued to sing and weave her way in and out through the men at the bar; one reached for her, bent her head back and kissed her on the neck, while another pulled at her arm, and, Farron on que, took hold of the man kissing her and knocked him to the floor. There followed a brawl until the director yelled, "Cut."

Farron reached for the man on the floor, "Sorry mate; hope I didn't hit you too hard!" But before the man could answer, Belle rushed up, threw her arms around Farron's neck, and kissed him. The newsman's camera flashed, and Belle ran to Captain Bill, looked into his eyes, and asked, "How did I do?" Bill blushed, "A little too convincing," he replied, "save it for me."

By now, everyone knew about the romance between Bill and Belle; some were envious, but not Farron; he was relieved. Fearing the photos of Belle with him would hit the news, he

wrote to Mary and explained.

He was right, of course, Mary had seen more than one photo of him with Belle in the Hollywood Reporter magazine. Blaine and Cecile had also seen the magazine and feared the publicity would upset Mary and cause her to lose the baby.

"No," Mary assured them she understood the pictures were necessary to promote the movie, "You must not worry about me, please. I admit it is not easy for me to know another woman is kissing my husband, but I know it is part of the script, and I have complete faith in Farron. He loves me and will have no other woman." And she was right, but prayed the filming would end soon; the baby must not be born while Farron was away.

While Mary dreamt of Farron, Belle wrapped herself around Bill, she kissed his neck, ran her hand across his broad chest, and wept, "J'aimeraid que tu n'es pas obliuge' d'aller an mer. J'ai peur!"

"My little dove," Bill replied, "you must stop speaking French, if you wish to make movies in the United States, you must speak English." His lips brushed against hers, "Think of this; if you become a star in America, I might never see you again?"

"And if you go to sea, a storm could take you away, and I might never see you again!"

"Stop! You must never say things like that. Never be afraid for me to fish the sea; it is bad luck. Never wave and wish me luck, that too is bad. You must always know I am safe. I know my

ship, my crew, and I know the Bering Sea waters. Be not afraid; I will return to you as long as you are in Alaska. But you will leave me and go to America, and who will you be with there?"

"I will have no one but you!"

"Aye, the lady does not speak the truth. You will have others, and you will forget me. I am not a fool; I am not your first, and I will not be your last."

Belle began to cry, "Tu penses que je suis bon marche'."

"No, sweet thing, I do not think you are cheap, but you have very hot blood, as do I."

"Bill, tu ne sais pas que je t'aime?"

"I would like to believe that you love me," he returned, "but you are going away, and the memory of me will fade. I, however, can never forget you because you have spoiled me for other women: Je t'aime, tres beaucoup little one. I also love you. My heart will ache when you leave for America."

"Si je rete veux-tu m'epouser?"

"Belle, you would give up acting for me, an old sea captain? You could never be happy away from the excitement, the attention, and the lights! With me, you would become a fish-wife. There would be no excitement! There would be much love and much waiting for your man to return. Is that what you want?. Maybe for a while, my love would be enough for you, but there would come a time when it would not, and you would hate me for marrying you. We must make the most of what we have now; we have no time to lose." Bill pulled Belle closer, kissed her gently, and made hungry, desperate love to her.

"Je ne peux pas te perdre," she whispered.

"No, you will never lose me," Bill answered, with the words weighing heavy on his mind and heart, "you must not think it or say it. We have a few more days in the saloon, and then we will go to the sea and search for Salmon. No women are allowed onboard the ship, but you will be here, and while we are out there in the icy waters, I will think of you snuggled down in our nice warm bed."

Belle began to cry, "Tiens moi et ne me laisse jamais partir."

Bill's arms tightened around her, and he whispered, "Do not cry, little one; we can never be apart."

"Vetre travail est dengereux?"

"There is danger in any man's work; I am an excellent helmsman, and I know these waters and my boat and crew better than anyone. Until you came along, my boat was my love; now I have two loves, and more reason to become a land-lover. Now, no more tears; kiss me and let me love you."

A few more days of filming in the saloon, and a few days of rest before going to sea, and Farron received a letter from Mary. She wrote: I cut out all the pictures of you and your leading lady. She is stunning; should I be jealous? I suppose I should, but I love

you so much, I know you would never leave me for an actress. I am anxious for this trip to end. I miss you. I need your arms around me, and I need to hear your voice. Darn, that place with no long-distance calls. It would be heaven to listen to you say you love me. I hope you get into a massive school of Salmon, with good weather, and end this darn trip so that you can be with me soon. Blaine and Cecile are taking good care of me. I love them, Farron. They gave me your room with all the pictures of you in it, plus I have your cell with your message and photos; all help me feel you are near. But there is an empty spot on your side of the bed; at night, I take the pillow, hold it in my arms, and pretend it is you. Your mother is teaching me to cook some of your favorite dishes, and I help her as much as possible with things around the house. In the meantime, Blaine fishes off the end of the pier, and every other day he catches fresh fish for our dinner. Think of me when you close your eyes at night, and I will close mine and think of you. I love you.

Farron carefully folded the letter, closed his eyes, and questioned why he had signed a binding contract with the studios. He had hoped for nothing but fishing, and here he was tied up in that damn saloon, pretending to be an actor. They could have hired Captain Armstrong; Bill was handsome, could do the job, and loved the leading lady. Too late now, he was stuck and had to stay with it. He closed his eyes and slept.

All but the last of the saloon scenes complete, come morning, if the weather allowed, they would set out to Sea. Farron awoke with a start, blood racing through his veins; this was it, he was finally going fishing.

Captain Bill Armstrong, the crew, cameramen, and Mort were waiting for him on the dock. Expecting to see Belle, he looked around, but she was not there. "Where's our leading lady?" he asked, and Mort replied, "Captain Armstrong said she would bring bad luck. You sea-going men are very superstitious."

"Yes, we are, Farron agreed, and it's damn cold here in April, but if we're going to catch King Salmon, this is the best time of year."

Captain Armstrong joined them, "The cameramen and crew are ready to leave, and Mort, your tag-along ship is waiting, so Farron, get aboard; we're going fishing."

Farron grinned, "I noticed your lady-love is not here to wave to you as we leave the dock."

"No, indeed not," Bill replied, "were she here, she would say something that would spook the men. We do not believe in farewell kisses or tears from our ladies; it brings bad luck and makes us think we might not return. Mort figured we should have something like that in the movie, but I told him if that took place, we would not leave the dock."

Farron and Captain Bill tipped their hats to Mort, turned away, and climbed onto the deck of the 'No Time To Lose,' a 58-foot vessel with a long clean deck, a boom with a power block, and net stacked on the back. Riding piggyback aboard the stern was a power skiff to assist with circling of floats while spreading the seining lines.

Captain Bill Armstrong directed Farron to the forward cabin or Bridge, and Bill took the wheel, the first mate yelled cast off, and, with an excellent, well-trained crew of six, they were on their way out of the harbor cutting through thin layers of ice.

A chilling spray of cold water made its way into the wheelhouse, and Bill allowed, "It may take us a day or so to find the Salmon. We might have to go up as far as Cape Newenham and fish between there and Cape Seniavin, or we might find a school of Salmon our first day out."

For a while, the two men stood silent, each with his thoughts. Bill was the first to speak, "Nice ship, isn't it?" Farron nodded, and Bill continued, "She's seen a lot of work and caught a lot of fish. I was born a fisherman; my dad was also a captain and ever so proud of his ship. He was a good strong man, my father, and a loving soul. He and my mother were true lovers. I guess I inherited his love of the sea, and for that matter, the way to love a woman." He smiled; his blue eyes searched the sea, and he thought of Belle's warm body against his, and continued, "Until I met Belle, there was not a woman who could touch my heart." He looked at Farron, "I suppose you think I'm a fool, but Belle holds my heart in her hands. She would like to quit this acting business and marry me, but I do not fool myself into believing I could make her happy away from all the excitement of acting and the promise of Hollywood."

"Don't be so sure, Bill; if she truly loves you, I think she would be happy and make you a good wife. And just think you could have a family and maybe a son to follow in your footsteps."

"Do you have a wife and family, and son?" Bill asked.

"I do not have a son. I have no children; I have a beautiful wife, Mary, whom I love more than life. She is content with what we have, and were it not for my father's persuasion; I would not have accepted this job of acting. I am not an actor; like yourself, Bill, I am a fisherman, and that's all I care to be. But my father is a ham actor, and if he were young, he would have done this. At one time, he owned a grain elevator in Indiana, but my mother suffers from acute asthma and could have died living in a damp climate. Doctors told my father he had to take her away, so he sold everything and moved to the west coast. Once there, he bought a boarding house near the ocean, and that's where I grew up. When I was not in school, my father taught me to fish," Farron chuckled, "and when I was about ten years old, I would catch surf-perch, put them in my little red wagon, and sell them to the Jewish people who came to the pier to buy fish; they loved buying from a little boy. I sold my perch cheap and wrapped them in the newspaper. When I grew up, I got a boat, a crew, and became a commercial fisherman." Farron stared out at the water and continued to talk, "I miss my wife, and ache to hear her voice. I wish this movie were over, and I could go home."

Captain Bill's eyes were on the fish finder, "We passed a small school of fish, but they were not Salmon. We can catch everything in this sea, and when we pull in the seining nets, you'll find a little of everything. Our primary industry is crabs; most of the other boats out here are Crabbers who target Dungeness crab, King crab, and Tanner crabs. The Crabbers make a good living, and it looks like they are all out here today. I think we'll head up toward Cape Newenham; between here and there, we should run into Salmon. It will take us about eighteen hours, but if we run into a couple of big schools, we'll let the nets out and go no farther." He called for John, the first mate, "Aye, Captain," John answered and waited for Bill to reply, "Go to the galley, get us some coffee, and, if the cook has anything sweet, get us something to go with the coffee. And, John, tell those camera Lads, while nothing's going on, they can get comfortable with the crew in the galley and have a bite to eat."

John laughed, "I don't think they'll be wantin' anythin'; they're a bit green in the gills."

"So soon?" Farron laughed, "Mort should have picked some men with sea-legs. What will they do if we get into a storm?"

"They'll stay where they are," John answered, "stretched out face down on their bunks. They are sick!"

Chapter 4

A bleary-eyed cameraman punched the fellow on the bunk next to his. "Feels like we've been out here forever, I thought we were supposed to get a few pictures and head back to Nome. Where the hell are we? All we needed was a few shots of that McClaine guy at the wheel. I think I'll go up and ask what's happening." Still, a bit green around the gills, Jim made his way to the wheelhouse, "Hay Captain," he shouted, "are we on our way back to land? We've got all the shots we need."

Bill looked at Farron, and they both laughed. "Well now, Bill said, "I'm glad to see you survived; you still look a little peaked. You better go to the gally and get yourself a cup of coffee and something to eat because it will be a while before we turn and head back to Nome. Right now, we are somewhere between Cape Newenham and Cape Seniavin, and we are about to lower the seining nets and circle the fish. You'll see a lot of action when we start that, so you better get your cameras ready." As he spoke, the wind blew icy spray through the wheelhouse, and the boat rose and fell between two twenty-foot waves.

"Holy Jesus!" Farron yelled, "That came up all of a sudden!"

Captain Armstrong struggling to hold the ship on course, shouted, "Tell the men to look alive! We're not far offshore; we're in for it! The sea is pushing me toward land." At the same time, the first mate shouted, "Captain, you've struck a rock. There's a hole in the hull, and we're taking on water, fast. We're going down!"

"Everyone, get in your life suits and lower the rafts," Captain shouted, as he signaled for help and gave their position. "Mayday! Mayday!"

Everyone scrambled, trying to get off the ship, and Captain shoved Farron out the door, "Get your survival jacket and get on a raft with the men."

"Are you coming?" Farron yelled back at him and tried to pull him away from the wheel.

"Yes! I'll be there," he shouted, and continued to send the message, "Mayday – Mayday! No Time To Lose! Mayday!"

Later, the Coast Guard rescued two crew members, and Farron, who, wearing survival suits, had spent hours on a life raft in high sea swells. Gale warnings of heavy freezing spray had been issued for the area between Cape Newenham and Cape Seniavin, but the warnings went unheard, and the ship, 'No Time

To Lose,' was caught and went down in the storm.

A week later, before eventually calling it off, rescuers continued to search for the missing crew members, the cameramen, and Captain Bill Armstrong.

Surviving members of the crew said, "Last we saw Captain, he was fighting his way out of the wheelhouse; the wind caught him, and he went down with the ship.

The news went hard on Mort, the kind of tragedy he never had cause to face. And when Belle heard the news, devastated, she screamed, "No! No! It's not true!" She collapsed at Mort's feet, and he yelled for help. An ambulance and Paramedics came, sedated Belle, and after Farron talked to the waiting reporters, he climbed into the ambulance and knelt next to Belle.

Belle, thrashing about with her eyes closed, whimpered, "Bill, Bill, Bill."

Farron reached for her, "He is not here, Belle. He is with God, and we can't bring him back."

Belle opened her eyes and stared at Farron, "I must! I must! Why? Why did this happen? I felt it in my heart and begged him not to go. I need him, Farron! I love him!" Tears streamed down her face, "What can I do? I don't want to live!"

Farron held her hand, "Belle, Bill told me how much he loved you. You were the only woman he ever loved. But Belle, we cannot foresee the future; our lives are in God's hands. Bill will always be with you. He wanted to make you his wife, but he was afraid he could not make you happy. He knew you loved acting and thought it was all you needed."

"I will never act again," Belle cried. "Never!"

"What will you do?" Farron asked.

Bell sobbed, and her body shook violently, "I don't know? I want to die and be with Bill; I want Bill."

Farron kissed her cheek and held her hand. "Belle, you are a strong woman, and if the Lord wanted you to die, you would die. The Lord has a reason for keeping you alive."

Belle's sobbing lessened, and she said, "Yes, you are right, there is a reason; I am carrying Bill's child in my belly. I will return to France, live with my mother, and have Bill's child. I wish he had known; I should have told him, but I was afraid. Now it's too late." Again, Belle began to sob uncontrollably, another sedative quieted her, and she slept.

Farron left the hospital, faced a dozen reporters, and answered their questions while his one thought was to get on a plane to the states. Mary, he had to see Mary; he needed to hold her and feel the comfort of her arms. Sure that she had heard the news, he was anxious for her to know he was safe.

Mary did not know he was safe; she listened to the news report and, thinking it was Farron, who had gone down with the ship, she collapsed.

"She'll lose the baby," Cecile cried, "call for an ambulance!"

In Blaine's hand was a telegram, and thinking it was to notify them of Farron's death, he shoved it in his pocket and reached for the phone. Noticing, Cecile asked what he was hiding. He shook his head as a warning, "I don't know," he said, "something I'll look at later when we know that Mary will be alright."

At the hospital, Blaine glanced at the telegram and said, "Cecile, take care of Mary; I have to go; this is urgent."

Puzzled, Cecile asked, "Is it more bad news?"

Blaine shook his head, "No! But I have to leave; prepare for

a surprise." The telegram stated; Will arrive, Los Angeles airport noon today. Blaine looked at his watch; he had forty-five minutes to get there, and when he arrived, the plane was on the ground.

Farron's saw Blaine and rushed to him. "Where's Mary?"

"Brace yourself, son. Mary is in the hospital."

"Oh, my God," Farron responded, "Why, for what?"

"She's alright; Cecile is with her. When we heard the news that the captain of the 'No Time To Lose' perished with the ship, Mary collapsed, and we took her to the hospital. I'll get you there as quickly as possible. Grab your luggage, and let's go; I'm in a no parking zone."

Farron pushed people aside to get his suitcase and rushed through the crowd to keep up with his dad. When they reached the car, both panting, Blaine said, "We made it and no ticked sticking to the windshield. I took a chance because I wanted to be there for you when you got off the plane. You have no idea how happy I am to see you alive. We have all missed you and depended on the Hollywood Reporter for news of the film, and you."

"The film," Farron grumbled, "My mistake, taking that job; it was hell from start to finish. We've got to get Mary well and home, then, I'll fill you in on everything. Mort is a hell-of-a nice producer, and his headaches have just begun. He is still in Alaska, taking care of all the unfinished business. He hated to see me leave but understood I'd had more than enough."

"And what about the money?" Blaine asked. "Will you still get paid?"

"I can't think of money, dad; here we are at the hospital; let's go see my wife."

They found Mary sitting up in bed and Cecile asleep in a chair beside her. When Mary saw Farron, she held out her arms and cried, "Thank God! You're alive! And you're here! Oh my Lord, can this be true?"

Farron rushed to her side and put his arms around her, "Now, what's this? What are you doing in this bed?"

Mary laughed, pushed the covers back, and put his hand on her belly, "Does this answer your question?"

"What?" Farron rubbed his hand across Mary's big round belly, "You mean," he stammered, "you are going to have a baby! You knew this before I left, didn't you? Why didn't you tell me?"

Mary pulled his face down to hers and kissed him, "Yes, my love, I knew, but I didn't want to worry you. I wanted you to go fishing in Alaska."

"Well, when, how long will it be before you have the baby?"

"Too long for you to start worrying. I was two months pregnant when you left; that was two months ago."

"It feels like six months. I've missed you so much, and if I had known you were carrying my child, I would not have gone."

"Exactly," Mary returned, "that's why I didn't tell you. Now,

as soon as they let me leave this place, we will go home, and you can tell us all about your harrowing experience."

"Home; you don't know how good that sounds. It's all I've dreamed of since the day I arrived in

Nome. Movies Hollywood are not for me. I am a fisherman, and that's all I ever want to be."

Little did Farron know that his days with films and Hollywood were not over. The ship went down, but the film did not go with it. Belle returned to France, and Farron returned home, but the wheels were still turning for Farron and his career.

Chapter 5

Farron expected a call from Mort, concerning the contract and what they were going to do about the money owed, and, as if he had willed it, the next day, a call came from Mort. "Farron, how are you? Did you think we had forgotten you? Sol and I would like to meet with you and discuss your contract and, of course, money. Where and when can we meet?"

"Mort! It's good to hear from you. I'm glad you're back in the states and still all in one piece! I wondered when I would see you; I expected a letter or notice of some kind. I am working, and my two helpers were happy to see me; we'll soon be heading out for some Bluefin Tuna."

"That's great, but I want to tell you, Farron. The studios and we have been in a bind over the loss of the ship and some of the film in Alaska. The studio does not want to sack the movie; they like the story, and you, and think they can salvage it. So, where would you like to meet with us?"

"Salvage the film? That's nuts, Mort! But, I would like to know if I will receive any of the money promised me in the contract. So, okay, I think tomorrow would be good. We can meet on the dock at Delaney's in Newport Beach. Do you remember Delaney's Restaurant? Be there at noon for lunch."

"Good; Sol, and I will be there. How's your family and your wife."

Farron laughed, "That's another story; I'm going to be a

father in about five more months. My wife was with child when I left for Alaska, but she didn't tell me. I arrived home to find her in the hospital; when she heard the captain of 'No Time To Lose' had drowned, she collapsed. Now that I'm home, she's happy, and I feel alive again."

"Fantastic," Mort exclaimed! I'm happy for you, but I deeply regret the loss of Captain Bill Armstrong; he too would have been a father; I say, would have because Belle lost their child. Bill was a great guy, and they were so much in love. I've heard little from her, but I know I will receive a request for money. She is an excellent actress, and although she vowed never to act again, she will! We'll talk about all this tomorrow at Delaney's."

"I am very sorry to hear Belle lost their child. The child was all she had left of Bill. That is sad news!"

Mort agreed, "But life goes on, Farron, as will Belle."

Farron said goodbye and turned to Mary, "Come here, my little fat wife; I love you, and we are so blessed."

"Farron, what brought that on?"

"Belle and Captain Bill Amstrong were deeply in love, had an affair, and Belle conceived. When Bill drowned, Belle wanted to die. Since then, the agony and stress caused her to lose their child."

Tears filled Mary's eyes, "And I came close to losing ours; yes, we are blessed!"

"Don't think about it," Farron begged. "Think about this; tomorrow, I meet with Mort and Sol at Delaney's, would you like to join us?"

"Thank you, Farron, that sounds important, and you know I don't care to be around when you are discussing business, but Blaine might like to join you. Ask him; he enjoys being needed."

The next morning Blaine grabbed a fishing rod, and Farron asked where he was going. "Oh," Blaine replied, "I thought I'd do a little surf-fishing this morning."

"Not today, dad. I would like you to join me for lunch at Delaney's. I'm meeting there with Mort and Sol to discuss the remainder of my contract."

"You bet, son! I'll just put this stuff away, change my clothes, and have a cup of coffee with you. Of course, I could fish off the dock until time for them to arrive, but I think I should look presentable when we meet."

"Well, your fishing duds are alright, but you do what you like. We have plenty of time for coffee and cinnamon rolls; it will take us about thirty minutes to drive to Delaney's from here. Parking is difficult at noon. I was supposed to take the boat and head out today; it's time for the Bluefin, but I called Jake and John and told them we would do it a day later. If you want, you can go with us. We'll be out a couple of days because we're going to search for the tuna around Channel Island and San Clemente. It's been a long time since you and I fished together."

Blaine beamed, "That's my boy! I'm glad you and Mary decided to live with us. Mary won't worry if she knows I'm with you. That little wife of yours worries too much, especially now, since the 'No Time To Lose' went down."

Cecile sat in a chair across from Blaine, "She's no different than I was when I was pregnant; it's normal for expectant mothers to worry."

Mary placed a plate of freshly cooked cinnamon rolls in the middle of the table. Yes, I will worry but not because you are fishing; it wouldn't matter where you were, Farron, I worry because I want you near when I have the baby. I hated it when you went off to Alaska, but I didn't want to hold you back. I'm sorry the trip ended so tragically, while at the same time, I'm glad you are home." She sat next to him, "Nothing like that can happen here, can it?"

Of course, Farron and Blaine both knew that all things are possible while on the ocean, but they both shook their head, and Farron replied, "No, nothing like that can happen in these waters. You are not to worry."

With an amused expression on her face, Cecile looked at both men and said, "We are fishermen's wives, and it is normal for us to worry. However, this is a boarding house, and Mary and I will not have much time to think of you out there cruising across the waves."

Farron swallowed the last bite of his cinnamon roll, gulped

down his coffee, and said, "Come on, Dad; got an appointment at Delaney's, and we need to leave stomach space for our lunch with Mort and Sol. Knowing how you like to eat, you might want a big platter of fried Shrimp."

Mary dropped what she was doing and ran for the bathroom.

Farron jumped up. "What's wrong? What's the matter?"

Cecile motioned for him to sit down, "Morning sickness, Farron. The mention of fried Shrimp did it." A faint smile crossed her lips, "Your father saw me do that a lot! I think you are going to have a son because that's what I did when I was carrying you. The thought of eating shrimp made Mary ill because she doesn't eat shellfish; it's against her religion."

A few minutes later, pale-faced, Mary returned and sat next to Farron. "Sorry, dear, I'm a little touchy these days, and the thought of eating shrimp made me sick."

"Maybe we shouldn't go! Maybe I should stay here near you."

Both ladies laughed, and Mary said, "That wouldn't change a thing."

Farron kissed her and turned to Blaine, "Come on, dad, let's get a move on it."

At Delaney's, they chose to sit at a table outside on the deck facing the cannery. "We can have a couple of beers while we wait, dad, and watch the action across the way. Look, there's a boat just pulling in." He waved to one of the men on the stern, "How'd you do?" he shouted.

The man on the boat waved back and answered in a loud voice, "Great! Farron, the Tuna are hitting!"

"Where?"

"Got these near Catalina! They were on the move, heading south."

Farron's friend was a sports fisherman, not commercial. He handlined the tuna and brought them to the cannery to be canned, with his name on the labels.

"I'm going out tomorrow," Farron shouted.

"Catch a bunch," his friend returned and held up a fish. "They are beauties."

"What's all the shouting about?" Mort asked as he and Sol arrived."

"Tuna! Albacore!" Farron replied. "Here have a seat, and Mort, Sol, meet my dad, Blaine McClaine."

Mort and Sol shook Blaine's hand and sat down at the table. "We couldn't have chosen a better day to meet, it's beautiful, and we are famished." Both men reached for menus stuck between the condiment bottle in the middle of the table, and at a glance, both said, "I'll have a large glass of grapefruit juice, scrambled eggs and lox with sour cream, on toast."

Blaine made an ugly face and said, "I'll have bacon, eggs, hash brown potatoes, and coffee. I don't know how you all can eat lox!"

Farron agreed with Blaine, "I'll have the same thing you're having, dad, but make mind sausage instead of bacon."

Sol burst out laughing, "I would rather have a shot of whiskey, pickled herring with marinated onions on a bun with sour cream, but I find nothing like that on this menu."

They all laughed, "I'm afraid not, Sol. I'm surprised you found lox and eggs; must have a Jewish cook in the kitchen."

Their breakfast served, Farron pointed toward the Cannery, "You see that boat, unloading fish; the fellow on the stern is a friend of mine. He caught enough Albacore out near the island to have them canned. We plan to go out tomorrow.

I've got to get to work and, if I'm lucky, make some money."

"Speaking of which," Mort said, "that's why Sol and I are here. The studio wants to salvage the film we started in Alaska, continuing it with you. The public knows only you as the captain and will not connect Captain Bill Armstrong with you."

"How is that possible?" Farron asked. "We don't have all the same people!"

"There were no outstanding characters in the crew, and the cameras were not focused on them, Farron, so no need to worry about that. You will get the total due on your contract, plus you can sell your catch to the cannery and double your money."

Farron shook his head, "Oh, I don't know about doubling my money; that's very iffy in this business. What about our leading lady? She went to France to have her baby, live with her mother, and vowed never to act again."

"We've talked to her, and she will come. Belle is an actress and will be until the day she dies. She grieves the loss of Bill and their child, but she is strong and must move on."

Farron was quiet, picturing the way Belle looked when he last saw her, devastated, and wanting to die. If she accepted the continuation of her part in the film, she indeed was more of a woman than he thought. Sighing heavily, he looked at Blaine, "Well, dad; it seems as if I'm going to be an actor whether or not I want. With the baby coming, I can use the money."

Blaine could not be happier, "I'll drink to that! Waitress, bring me a beer."

Sol smacked his lips over his eggs and lox, "Make that four, waitress. I think we all need a drink."

"You know, son; I think you should give this acting business a little more thought. It is a lucrative business, and if you are a success in this film, there's no telling how far you can go. It isn't as if you would give up fishing; you can always fish. You just said the fishing business is iffy; some years are good, and others not so good."

Farron grinned at Sol and Mort, "If my dad were young, he would be an actor."

"Well," Mort added, "he has a point. You are a big, good-looking guy, and without trying, you have a very natural delivery. There might be a new world out there for you. But remember, if it happens, I'm your producer."

Sol added, "And I'm your agent."

Farron sipped on a beer and watched his friend pull his boat away from the dock in front of the cannery. "Now, see that boat; it is very much like mine. It is much different from the 'No Time To Lose.' How will you explain that when you continue with the film's plot? I have a Sportfishing powerboat with a flying bridge. We will have lines in the water because I am going for the Bluefin Tuna."

"That is up to the scriptwriters, Farron. I'm sure they will find a way to explain why you are now in the Pacific waters off California. However, you might need to return to Nome for a send-off showing you leaving for the coast. Perhaps the difference in the size of your boat will be an improvement with you on the flying-bridge."

Excited, Blaine added, "Don't think of this as work, Farron; think of it as an adventure, and welcome in a new way of life."

"My father," Farron exclaimed, "should be in the movies."

"Well, maybe we can find a way to work him into a few shots. If this works, and I feel sure it will, your dad can be on the boat with you in some of the fishing shots, and maybe more! He looks amazingly like Bill Armstrong and could be part of your Alaskan crew. All this depends on the script and where the writers go with it. They might decide to end it with you and Belle leaving port as a happy couple heading out to sea. They can put Belle's name on the stern. That sounds like a quick and easy finish to the Alaskan adventure, don't you think? I will suggest that to the writers."

Sol laughed, "Mort always tells the writers what he thinks; sometimes they agree, and sometimes they tell him to get lost."

Chapter 6

Mary disliked the idea of Farron returning to Nome, Alaska, even for a week. "Will you be going out to sea," she asked, "I don't want you fishing the Bering Straits again."

Farron assured Mary that there would be no fishing, "It's a short bit added to the film to explain why I, the captain, returned to the states. The leading lady will also be there; she is in France now, but will return to finish the film."

Without question, Belle was at the airport in Nome awaiting their arrival; she saw Farron, ran to him, threw her arms around him, cameras clicked, Farron, kissed her, and felt his heart sink; another thing to upset Mary.

The departure scene for the filming in Nome, Alaska, went quickly with Farron and Belle's dramatic performances over the horrific sinking of the 'No Time To Lose.'

Watching Belle closely, Farron expected to see her collapse, and he confessed, "I thought you would never act again, Belle, especially in a scene like this."

"Nor did I, Farron, but one must live. Acting is the only thing I know how to do. I am without Bill, and I am without our baby; I must make money to support myself and my mother. Living in France is not cheap. We have an apartment on the Left Bank, and my rent is three thousand dollars a month. Fortunately, we, I and my mother saved what we could, but our money cannot last forever. I need to make this movie, and if I am successful, I will remain in Hollywood and make many more. I will move to the United States and bring my mother to live with me. Life is indefinable! Just when everything is perfect, God changes the course of our existence. Bill was the first and only man I ever loved; with him, my life was beautiful and complete; now, my life is empty, finished, and I have nothing left for which to live except my mother, an aching heart, and acting."

Farron put his arms around Belle, "Your life is not over, Belle. When we lose the one we love most in this world, we think we want to die and be with them, but we do not die because that is not our decision; our lives are in God's hands. Also, believe it or not, we continue to live because we want to see the light of day. At first, we are angry and question why the Lord chose to take our loved one, but Belle, the love we shared with another, will always live within us. You will never again see Bill's face or feel his arms around you except in your dreams and your memory. But when you think of him, know that he is in a better place because he no longer has the worries of the world and survival to face. You still have your mother, and the Lord willing you will find someone to love again."

Belle kissed Farron, "You are so kind and understanding; I am glad we met."

"Now, my dear, we must think of the future. When we reach Los Angeles, did Mort make living arrangements for you?"

Alarmed, Belle replied, "No! Will it be difficult for me to find an apartment in Hollywood? Someone must help me."

"I'm sure that in time you will find something, but Belle, for now, you will need a place to stay, and since Mort has not done this for you, I think you must stay with my wife, my father and mother, and me. My father owns an old but large two-story boarding house on the beach. Now, such places are called Bed and Breakfast apartments. It is not fancy; it passes all the city's requirements, is safe, and like no other place you have seen, and it will cost you nothing for three rooms. For those who want breakfast, we serve in the dining room; my wife and mother do the cooking. Everyone knows everyone, and we are like one big happy family."

Tears streamed down Belle's face, "I will try to be happy, Farron. You are very kind, but I am without Bill, and without him, how can I be happy? No one can replace Bill; he was gentle, loving, and he loved me. He understood me and my needs. Do not try to predict my future because, Farron, there will never be another man for me. You have an understanding, loving heart, and I have never known such kindness. Your offer to live in your father and mother's apartment building takes my breath away, and of course, I accept your offer, but I must pay the same as others." She held out her hand and asked, "Are the three rooms large enough for two people? Perhaps, if I am a success, I can bring my mother to America."

Farron laughed, "Yes, the three rooms are big enough for two, but Belle, if you make films in America, you will want a home or a luxury apartment in Bel Air, and it will cost as much or more than your apartment in France. Of course, when you become a very famous star, you will buy a home. And then who knows? You might meet someone, fall in love, marry, and live in a Hollywood mansion." He watched the expression in Belle's eyes as she shook her head and sighed. "For now, however, you will live a simple life in the home of a fisherman. Mary and I own a little house on the beach, but while I was away, Mary moved in with mom and dad, and we have since rented our home to an old man and woman who love to surf fish. My wife will meet us at the airport; she is beautiful, shy, and pregnant. I will soon be a father."

As expected, Mary was waiting, and when she saw Belle, so beautiful and thin, she felt a tinge of jealousy. Her hand went to her belly, "I am so pleased to make your acquaintance," she said, and reached for Belle's hand, "you are beautiful, just like your pictures," and turning with tears of excitement in her eyes, her arms went around Farron, "I'm so glad you are home!"

Farron pulled her to him, "Not nearly as glad as I am to be home! We were lucky; the filming went smoothly and quickly." He kissed her and held her at arm's length, "and how is my expectant mother feeling? Have you had any problems while I was gone?"

Mary blushed and giggled, "Just a little morning sickness, and you know what Cecile says about that. Now come on, Cecile and Blaine are waiting; I'm parked right in front of the entrance, and we don't want a ticket. You drive, I don't fit too well behind

the wheel and traffic is fierce."

As they made their way down the coast, Farron told Mary that Belle was to live with them, and why. "Is everything rented, or do we have an empty apartment."

Mary tried turning to look at Belle, who was sitting in the back seat, "Belle, how wonderful! Having you with us should be fun; I will get a chance to see actors rehearse."

Farron laughed, "I don't think we will be doing much of that. The way Mort talked, we are about through with the film."

"Well, Belle, you are in luck, a couple from the east left a few days ago, and we have a three-room apartment on the second floor. There is no elevator, so you must climb the stairs. It is a lovely apartment with a balcony where you can sit and enjoy the view and sea breeze."

Belle leaned forward and smiled, "It sounds wonderful, not unlike the apartment my mother and I have in France."

Again, Farron laughed, "I hardly think it will compare!"

"No matter," Belle replied, "I appreciate your kindness, and when possible, I will bring my mother to America. But Mary, do you climb the stairs in your condition?"

"Not often!"

"You should not do it at all. Please allow me to clean and care for my apartment; do not climb the stairs. If I find I need something, I will come to you. Are there phones in the rooms?"

"Yes, but all calls come through the office, and we transfer them from there to the rooms and apartments. Also, if you wish to talk with us, there is an intercom on the wall near the door. The apartments are not modern; things are oldfashioned."

Farron parked in front of the apartment building, helped the ladies out of the car, and grabbed Belle's one piece of luggage. Belle breathed in the fresh air, looked out at the ocean, and exclaimed, "Mon Dieu c'est beau!" And then in English, she said, "This is beautiful, I am in heaven. How can I ever thank you?"

"We will enter through the kitchen door, Belle; that's where we will find my mother and father. She will be cooking, and he will be eating." Farron was right, and Cecile turned away from the stove, wiped her hands on her apron, and went straight to Belle.

"Welcome! I know you are Belle; you look just like your pictures." She punched Blaine on the shoulder, "Blaine, get your nose out of that newspaper, we have company."

"Oh, sorry!" He set his cup on the table, rose from his chair, and smiling, faced Belle, "Did you have a pleasant flight," he asked?"

Belle's face lost color, and for a moment, she stammered, "My God, am I seeing a ghost? Is this your father, Farron? He looks like Bill!"

Embarrassed, Farron replied, "I'm sorry, Belle, I should have

warned you, but I forgot. When I first met Bill, I, too, was taken aback by the resemblance."

Blaine looking puzzled, asked, "What's going on?" Without waiting for an explanation, he continued and reached for Belle's hand, "Lovely lady, I hope my appearance does not offend you."

Recovering, Belle smiled and removed her hand from his, "Your looks do not offend me, but they did startle me. I was deeply in love with the captain of the 'No Time To Lose,' and I lost him when the ship went down." Tears streamed down her face. "You look so much like him, for a moment, I thought he was alive. Now I will live here in this house with you and your wife, and every day I will be reminded."

"If the memory will be too much for you," Blaine offered, "I will make an effort to stay out of your way. We want you to be happy; everyone who lives with us is happy."

"Oh, no, please do not make yourself scarce; seeing you makes me think Bill is sending me messages. When you see the movie, you will understand why your appearance shocked me. He, of course, was French, and you are?"

"I am Scotch, and my lovely wife, Cecile, is Irish. You will eat a lot of Irish-delights; Irish Beef Stew with Crusty bread, sea-food chowder, corned beef-n-cabbage, Apple walnut slaw, date pecan bread, apple cake, and I could go on, but I am getting hungry. Do you cook?"

"I? No, just a little, but my mother is famous for her French

cooking. If I bring her, she will enjoy being in the kitchen with Cecile. She must come; I am so excited! Now, if you will show me to my apartment."

Mary started for the stairs, and Farron stopped her. "No, my little round wife, you will not climb the stairs, I will take her." He stepped in front of Belle, "Follow me."

They reached the landing, and Belle stopped to breathe, "I should not be out of breath," she said, "the stairs in France are steeper."

Farron opened the door to Belle's apartment. She took one step inside, rushed to the folding doors leading onto the balcony, opened them, and stepped outside. Farron followed and stood beside her; one of her arms went around his waist, and she exclaimed, "This is magnificent!" She sucked in the fresh air, "Look at this! What a view; I see a sailboat on the ocean. I must talk to my mother, tell her where I am staying, and that I want her here with me. I will take pictures from this balcony and send them to her. She will love it, and she will love that it is not new and modern. This apartment could be in France, except it needs ornate wrought-iron railings. I don't care about making movies; I can get work doing something else. Oh, Farron, I feel like a new person." She looked around the rooms at the furniture and shyly asked, "Do you think that Blaine and Cecile would mind if I were to change the furniture in this apartment? If they don't mind, I will buy French Provincial furniture, make everything look like our apartment in France, and my mother will feel at home."

Farron began to laugh; it looked as if Belle was here to stay. "Belle, you can do anything you like to this apartment; however, I think you have forgotten that you are an actress, and if you make films, you will want to move to Hollywood."

"Reste a' savoir!" Belle giggled and asked, "You think I will work in Hollywood? That remains to be seen." She wandered from room to room, smiling, "I know exactly what to do with these rooms; in no time, it will look like Paris. I can hardly wait." Belle reached for the phone on the wall, "May I call my mother now?"

"You can, Belle, but it would be easier for you to make the call from the downstairs office; all the calls go through the office. I know it's a strange system, but if you want a direct line, we can call the phone company; then, you can buy a French Phone, have it installed, and have a separate line into your apartment."

"Yes, yes, I will do that when I buy the furniture for these rooms." Belle kissed Farron on the lips, and he pulled away. "Oh," Belle said, "I am sorry, please don't misunderstand my kiss; I am so excited I could kiss everyone."

Shaken, he replied, "I understand, but please don't do anything like that in front of Mary."

"But Farron," Belle said, "Mary will see me kiss you when we are filming!"

"I know, and she won't like that either, Bell. Don't forget she is pregnant, and every lady with a flat belly is a threat to her."

Belle laughed, "You are right, Farron; I didn't think about that. Now, we go downstairs, and I will call my mother. She will be so excited."

They found Mary and Cecile in the kitchen and Blaine having a cup of coffee and a piece of pie. "You were gone a long time," Mary said, "I was about to send Blaine after you."

Farron put his arms around Mary, "Yes, we were because Belle loves the apartment and the view, and wants to bring her mother here as soon as possible. Please take her into the office and let her use the phone to call Paris."

Blaine put his fork down and said, "I'll be happy to show you into the office."

Cecile turned and waved a spoon at him, "You sit back down and finish your pie," she laughed, "he can't resist beautiful women; he's an old dog but still has the idea in his head."

Blaine grinned, "After all these years, it's nice to see my wife is still jealous."

Mary looked at Farron, "For God's sake, Farron, take Belle in and help her make her call. It will go through the switchboard, Belle, and charged to your apartment."

"You come with us," Belle urged, "and you can say hello to my mother, Juliette. She speaks a little English and will understand; however, her accent might make it difficult for you to follow." Belle held the phone close to her ear, and tears ran down her face as she heard her mother's voice, "Maman c'est

moi ton enfant capricieux." Then, through tears and laughter, French words of joy filled the room." Mary and Farron shrugged their shoulders and sat listening. Finally, Belle announced, "Je te pre'sente mon amie," and she handed the phone to Mary, "Listen, my mother will say hello."

Mary took the phone and listened to a barrage of English and French words, smiled, and handed the phone to Farron; he laughed and gave the phone to Belle. Belle laughed, and to her mother said, "J'expliqerai, Maman; tu as parlet trop vite pour eux. Je t'aime et je t'enverrai rapidemente. Au revoir mon amour!" Bell placed the phone on the receiver, wiped away her tears, and said, "Thank you! My mother was thrilled to hear my voice, and she will probably start packing her things right this minute. She has never been out of France, not even to England; she married a baker and worked with him until he died; she then took over the bakery and until recently continued to work. I talked her into selling the bakery, and now she does nothing but sits at home and visits with her friends. This trip will give her a new life."

Cecile added, "It will be good for me too. She can help me with my cooking. Mary helps, but she has little experience, and with the baby coming, she will not want to be in the Kitchen."

"I can help; I am not a great cook like my mother, but I can cook a little," Belle replied, "and I can make French pastries."

Everyone laughed, and Mary patted her belly, "I felt a little movement; do you think the baby can hear my thoughts? I was mentally tasing French Eclairs filled with sweet flavored cream."

Farron held out his arms, "Bring that little body over here, sit on my lap and have a piece of Apple pie with whipped cream on the top."

"Silly, I can't sit on your lap; I will sit next to you and have the pie."

Cecile placed a medium-sized piece of the pie in front of Mary and topped it with whipped cream. Mary frowned, "Is that all I get? Don't forget; I'm feeding two!" They all laughed, and she continued, "Forgive me for changing the subject, but when do you think they will start filming?"

"You would mention that," Farron complained, "I believe Mort said it would be this coming week; I'm praying for rain or something so that we can put it off a while longer."

"Not I," Belle exclaimed, "I want to get it done before my mother arrives! Juliette is like Blaine; she would want to be in on the action. If they allowed women on the boats, she would be there, and she is beautiful!"

"This is not Alaska, Belle," Farron said, "we allow women on the boat; lots of women fish for the big ones. If we go for the Bluefin

Tuna, they are big, hefty fish, and when someone has a hookup, the captain maneuvers the boat back and forth to help bring the fish in. And Belle, they might get a picture of you with one on the line."

Excited, Belle exclaimed, "Really! Can I fish in the next

scenes? Le Destin peut-il me porter une telle chance! My God! Fate has brought me such luck! I am so happy!"

"Now wait, Belle. We don't know what the script is going to do with us. I know Mort wants us to go fishing, but we do not know if he will include you. He might want to leave you on the dock, waving goodbye."

"No, no, no," Belle returned, morosely, "he cannot do that to me; it would be bad luck." She could hear Bill's voice; you cannot wave goodbye; it would bring bad luck." Tears came into her eyes; she turned away and excused herself.

"Wait, Belle," Farron called after her, "this is a different kind of fishing, and this is a different country. Here, you can go with me, and you can fish; that is if the script calls for it." Too late,

Farron's words went unheard as Belle left the room.

"Now, what was that all about?" Blaine asked, and Farron explained.

Chapter 7

Belle wasted no time, "My mother will be here in three weeks. She wanted to come sooner but said she had too much business to clear up before leaving France. I must get everything ready for her arrival. May I paint the balcony railings and hang some potted flowers on them? And one on the wall behind my small three-piece Bistro set? It has cushioned chairs and is very comfortable for us to sit at the little table while having tea or a glass of wine. Also, I would like to remove the furniture in all three rooms and replace it with French Provincial."

Mary looked at Cecile, and Cecile replied, "You can do anything you like, Belle," and Mary added, "I wish I could climb the stairs; if I could, I would help you."

"Oh, Mary, Cecile, thank you! I am blessed to live with such beautiful friends. I will start today."

By the end of the week, with the furniture in Belle's three rooms removed and replaced with French furniture, the apartment looked like one in Paris. Colorful wallpaper covered the walls, and from ceiling to floor, shuttered windows opened onto a sunny balcony with hanging flowers. Belle held her cell phone in front of Mary, "Look at these pictures I took of my apartment. I know you cannot climb the stairs, and I thought you would like to see what I have done."

Mary's viewed the pictures, one by one, laughed," When I saw all the action going on up and down the stairs, I could not

visualize what was going on up there. You have no idea how many times I was tempted to climb and look. I suspect when some of our other guests see what you have done, they will want to change things."

Until now, Farron had said nothing, "I doubt that honey; not all can afford to redecorate, and I suspect that Belle has spent most of her earnings from the film."

Bell winked at Mary, "Not quite," she said, "when I buy, I bargain, and I bought everything for less than advertised. In France, we never pay full price."

Cecile poured everyone a cup of coffee and placed an upsidedown pineapple cake in the middle of the table. "This is Blaine's favorite, and I think you are all due for a little snack. I know the expectant mother is hungry."

Mary rubbed her hand across her belly, smiled at Farron, and said, "I am, and so is the baby." Directing her words to Belle, she moaned, "I do wish I could see the apartment."

Four voices chimed, "No, you don't! After the baby comes, you can go up and sit on the balcony with Belle and her mother."

Their happy gathering was interrupted with a phone call; Farron listened, hung up the receiver, and laughed, "It's not over til' it's over. That was the phone company; they are on their way to install a phone in your apartment, Belle. Did you buy a phone?"

"Indeed, I did. I have an antique ornate floral pink and white

European-style villa home phone. It is beautiful! Oh, I can hardly wait for my mother to arrive! Mary, when you looked at the photos on my cell phone, did you not notice a French fixture on the stand next to the bed."

Mary held out her hand, "Let me look at the pictures again." She saw the phone and asked, "Belle, does your apartment make you feel you are now in France?"

"It does Mary, and Juliette, my mother, will feel right at home, especially when she sits on the balcony and looks out at the water."

"Oh, can you see the water from your apartment in France?"

Belle smiled, "No, we cannot see the River Seine, but we have a marvelous view of our street-artists and markets bustling with activity. We, two lone ladies, need to see and feel action around us. We know many people, and often while sitting on our balcony, they pass by, stop, look up at us, and we invite them up for a glass of Cabernet Sauvignon and a bite of baked Brie with figs and nuts." Belle looked around the table at everyone, "Paris is beautiful, and I will miss it, but not as much once me're, our loving word for mother, arrives."

The phone men arrived, and one very tall, handsome man admiringly eyed Belle. "Are you Miss Belle Fauche'?"

Belle blushed, and for a moment, thoughts of Bill escaped her. "I am," she said, coquettishly, "follow me, my apartment is

upstairs. I trust that will not cause a problem?"

"None whatever," he replied and fell in behind her. "You have an accent; are you French?"

"Oui, but of course, I hope I am not too difficult to understand!"

"Not at all," he answered. "I am of French descent; my name is Philip Dubois. I grew up in the state of Louisiana, as do many other Frenchmen."

"Alors tu parles Francais?"

"No, I do not speak French," he smiled seductively, "but I know how to make love like a Frenchman!"

They had reached the top of the stairs and stood in front of her door; she turned, "And you are as fresh as a Frenchman." She opened the door, and they stepped inside; he stopped, glanced around the rooms, and exclaimed, "This apartment looks like the pages out of a magazine!"

"You like?" Belle asked.

He exclaimed, "I would never have guessed there would be anything like this in the rooms of this building!"

"I have a French phone," Belle pointed to the phone on the stand next to her bed, "will I be able to use it?"

"Of course! I will connect it, but is it the only phone you have? He walked out onto the balcony, "This is fantastic! Would

you like to have another phone here?"

"I would love to have a phone on the balcony, but I only bought this one."

"Permit me," he replied, "I have a French phone in the truck that someone decided they did not want. It is not as ornate as the one you have, but it is antique and is French; would you like to have it?"

"Philip, you are too kind, but of course, I would love to have your phone; how much will it cost?"

Philip smiled, "For you, it will cost nothing."

"Oh, merci," Belle returned. "Nevertheless, in return, I must do something for you! Please, while you are doing your work, I will get a bottle of wine, some cheese, and when you have finished, if you have the time, we can sit on the balcony, sip a glass of wine, and get acquainted."

Grinning, and with a sparkle in his dark brown eyes, he assured her, "I will have the time."

As Philip worked, Belle rushed down the stairs and entered the kitchen, "Cecile, do we have any wine and cheese?"

Farron got up, went to a cabinet, and handed her a bottle of Louis Jadot Beaujolais; we just happen to have several different kinds of wine. My father likes wine. And with an amused expression on his face, "Are you entertaining?"

Belle blushed, "Yes. The gentleman is so kind; he has given

me an extra phone, and I thought I should reward him." She reached in the frigidaire, got a square of cheese. "Cecile, do you mind if I cut a few squares off of this."

Cecile smiled at Farron and answered, "Please take as much as you like, and also a few crackers and nuts."

Belle quickly took the wine and cheese to her apartment, placed everything on the little table between the two chairs, returned to the room, and watched Philip work. He had stirred something inside her that she never thought she would feel again; after all, she was still alive!

As they sat and sipped their wine, Philip mused, "This was my lucky day; here I sit with a beautiful lady sipping wine and enjoying the ocean view from her balcony. Tell me, what are you doing in the United States? What brought you here?"

"I am an actress, Philip. I worked on a film in Alaska, and something happened that did not allow us to finish it. I had hoped to get into the movies in Hollywood, but my dreams ended because of a terrible shipwreck on the Bering Sea." She quieted and held back tears as she felt Bill's arms around her. "However, despite the accident, the producer thinks we can complete the film here. The gentleman, Farron McClaine, whom you met downstairs, is a fisherman, not an actor, but he too was in the movie." Belle sighed, "To make a long story short, we are going to complete the movie here."

Philip filled his glass again with wine, "You are an actress; I

should have known. But why do you live here? Why are you not in Hollywood?"

"When the producer brought me to the states, he did not arrange or rent an apartment for me. Farron asked if I would like to live with him and his family, and since I had no place to go, I accepted. They are lovely people; he is very much in love with his wife, Mary, and she will soon have his child. I feel so blessed to have these new loving friends."

Philip nodded, "And I am blessed because I met you. Little did I know when I left home this morning, I would meet someone with whom I would fall in love."

Belle laughed, "You may be American born, but you are truly French! Why do you think you love me?"

"At first glance, I knew. How could I not love you? You are beautiful and desirable and set my blood on fire. God must have planned our meeting; this can not be the only time I will see you. Tell me that you will see me again."

Belle reached for his hand and held it in hers, "We will meet again and again. If necessary, I will have trouble with my phones, and you will return to fix them," she chuckled.

"No, Belle, you will have no trouble with your phones; I will come for you, and we will dine together, and when we each have time to play, we will go to the beach, we will lunch on the pier, and we will take a boat to Catalina Island,

and spend a few nights in one of the hotels with views of the water."

"You are too quick, Philip, and you excite me, but we cannot do all the things you suggest. I will not spend nights with you in a hotel in Catalina. There are things you must know about me; things I think will make you see me differently."

Philip shook his head, "You can tell me nothing that will cause me to think differently of you; nothing."

"I am afraid I can. I had not intended to tell you this, but you are so rash; so quick, you disregard the consequences, the risk, of being hurt."

Philip frowned, "And how, sweet thing, can you hurt me?"

Contemplating the outcome of what she must tell Philip, Belle hesitated. "I have loved, Philip, and lost. I had a child; I lost the child's father to the sea, and I miscarried his child. When I lost my lover, I wanted to die, but the Lord would not allow that. I swore I would never love again, never. And now, I am faced with the truth about myself; I am a coward, and I no longer want to die. Because of you, I want to live. As I have told you, I came to the United States because the producer of the film we were making in Alaska believes we can complete the movie here."

Taken aback by her words, Philip sat down and held his head in his hands. "You were in love, and you had a child; my God, I never could have guessed!" He pulled her onto his lap and kissed her neck, "Do you think that anything you've said can change the way I feel about you? It only makes me love you more. You have lived through Hell, and you survived. And Belle,

my feelings for you are real; I am not trying to seduce you. We can go to Catalina, stay in the hotel, and have separate rooms. You will find the island beautiful, with ocean waves washing ashore whispering, peace." Philip kissed Belle again, "Now tell me, "When does this movie-making business begin?"

Belle stood up and faced Philip with love-filled eyes, "I will know in a day or so when we meet with the producer. Don't be impatient," she giggled, "you have my phone number."

Philip looked at his watch, "Oh God, I'm late to my other job!" He tossed his wine back, stood up, pulled Belle to him, kissed her, and she returned his kiss. "Tonight," he said, "I will come for you, and we will dine in Newport

Beach at the Fogo De Chao Steak House. I think you will love it."

"I'm sure I will," she returned, "after all, I am dining with Louis Jourdan!"

"Others have called me that, but no, you are dining with Philip Dubois, don't confuse me with someone else." He laughed and left.

Chapter 8

Two days later, Mort and Sol met with Farron and Belle in the kitchen of the boarding house. Farron introduced them to Cecile, and glanced at Blaine, "I believe you've met my dad; please have a seat, and if there is anything you would like, coffee, tea, booze, or food, just say the word, and Cecile, my mother will get it for you."

Sol glanced at Mort, "Well Mort isn't this grand? I thought we would be sitting at a table on the dock again." He looked at Cecile, "I can't speak for Mort, but if you have a little fresh-squeezed orange juice, I will skip the coffee, and, if possible, I would love French-toast with syrup and fruit."

Grinning, Mort added, "Yes, dear lady, I'll have the same."

Blaine added to the request, "You know what I like, honey; I'll have coffee, bacon, eggs, toast, and jelly. These fellows don't know it, but I might join them and Farron on the search for Bluefin Tuna. I've been aching to do a little fishing with my boy."

Farron added, "Mort, Sol, I'm glad to see you are comfortable in our humble surroundings, and mom is a great cook. You will find this better than breakfast on the pier. Of course, you know my dad is anxious to get in front of your cameras."

Mort smacked his lips over the French-toast and agreed. "When do you think we can start? I know Belle has arrived in the states; have you talked with her? If so, have you filled her in on things?" He handed Farron a couple of scripts; there's not much to these because you will be fishing. Is it possible for Belle to be on the boat with you?"

"Yes, I told Belle, and she was surprised to hear we are not all as superstitious as the fishermen in Alaska. If you like, I will ring her apartment and have her join us for breakfast."

Surprised, Mort asked, "Belle lives here with you?"

"Oh, I felt sure you knew! When she arrived and found that you had not arranged a place for her to stay, I offered her an apartment, and she accepted. I thought she called you."

"Yes, she did but failed to say she was living with you. She gave me a post office box number and asked that I send a check to that address. She is a cagey little one, isn't she?"

A voice came from the doorway, "No, I am not; at that time, I thought I should have a post-office box." She stood next to Cecile, "I'm going to have a cup of coffee, a bowl of fruit, and two slices of wheat toast, and I'll get it." She brought her coffee to the table and sat looking at the men. "I looked over the few lines that are in the script, and to me, it seems as if the entire thing is going to be, as you say, adlib,

and this time, I will be on the ship."

Farron interrupted, "We can not call it a ship, Belle because it is a Sports-fishing craft; a thirty-three foot Sports fisherman with a Fly Bridge, and we do not have a large crew. There will be Blaine and two other men plus a cameraman, and I hope that guy has sea legs because we might be in some very rough waters." Noticing a concerned expression in Belle's eyes, he continued, "Yes, Belle, we might be in some very rough seas; are you prone to motion sickness?"

Belle nervously answered, "I don't know?"

"Well," Farron warned, "it will not take long for us to find out. We can take you on a little test trip and drift outside the harbor in the trough between waves, and if you don't look to the shore, you might get sick; if so, you will take a Dramamine and lie face down on a bunk below,"

"Oh God," Belle exclaimed, "thinking about it makes me sick!"

Mort laughed, "You are an actress, and we won't have a stand-in for this, but if you think you can not do it, we can leave you onshore."

"No, no, no, Mort, I must be a part of all the action."

"I want you to think this over carefully, Belle, because if we find the Bluefin Tuna, we will have to fight the fish, and if it is a huge one, it could take two or more hours to bring it in, and once hooked, the work begins; the first thirty minutes after the catch

is crucial, and for you, if you are with us, very scary." Farron chuckled, "I know you won't know what I'm talking about, but I must tell you what will happen once we catch a Bluefin Tuna. We bring the fish and leader up to the boat, gaff the fish in the head area, and get it swimming alongside the boat. In time, it will lie on its side, exhausted. After gaffing the tuna, we will slip a tail rope over the tail and, using a second gaff, pick it up; then, we cut the leader, remove the hook, and sink a head hook through the lower jaw and start swimming the fish from its head, behind the boat. We will try to swim the fish for about twenty minutes until its color returns, and then tow it by the tail and bleed it out. While dragging the fish, we rake its gills with a gaff or harpoon, and once the blood flow slows and the fish shows little movement, we haul it onto the deck and quickly dress it; a very messy process. After that, we cool it and cram the body cavity with as much tightly packed crushed ice as possible. Next, we put the carcass into a cooler bag packed in a bed of ice, and we shove the bag into my below-deck cooler."

Mort, Sol, and Belle said nothing; each sat with mouth opened and in amazement stared at Farron. He grinned and looked at Belle, "Now, are you sure you want to be part of that scene?"

Belle shook her head from side to side, "No, I do not; the thought of all that blood and guts makes me want to throw-up. I will never eat tuna again! What a horrible way to kill!"

Mort added, "Farron, you say you would rather fish than

Act? Oy vey! I could never be a fisherman. But if you catch a big one, it will make a hell of a great action-packed movie."

"Yes, there will be lots of action as we will be in some rough seas down around San Clemente Island or offshore below the Mexican border. I don't expect you to understand why I love fishing; it is just a part of me. When I am out there on the water, I feel close to our maker, and I am at peace with the world."

Belle grunted, "I don't think the way you kill and mistreat a big fish is very Godly!"

"Ah, but Belle, our Lord, helped the fishermen. Think, and remember, when Christ was near the Sea of Galilee, he told the fishermen on which side of the boat to cast their nets? Any kind of killing is unpleasant, but if you are going to eat meat, fish, fowl, or seafood, it must die, and if that makes you unhappy, then you can become a vegetarian. But let me tell you, women also fish for the big ones, and they are not skittish."

Belle kicked it around in her mind and muttered, "I guess? But I am not going with you when you fish for that Bluefin Tuna. I don't want to see a fish tortured, and I don't want to see the guts on the deck; it makes me sick to think of it."

"It didn't do much for my breakfast either," Sol said, "let's get out of here Mort and tell the scriptwriters how to catch a Bluefin Tuna."

"They probably have some stock-film on it already, but not with our man in it, and I think we will need Belle, even if it is just

here in the harbor as they are leaving, and on their return." Mort rose from his chair, "We should be on our way," he turned to Cecile, "I thank you for a delicious breakfast and the delightful company."

Cecile thanked him, "My pleasure to cook for men who enjoy eating, you must come for dinner one night. We serve dinner in the dining room, but there is no menu; you eat that which I am serving for the night. Everyone who lives with us joins in for dinner unless they have other plans. The dining room is the same as dining in a restaurant; all have individual tables. Nearly everyone comes, and Mary helps me serve. Most of the people who live with us are seniors, but not too old to enjoy a few drinks and jokes. Our group and the way they live and feel about life would make an interesting movie." She laughed.

"That's not a bad idea! Sol, maybe we could include it in the fishing film? Farron, our star, his life with his dad and mom, and all the colorful characters in the boarding house. Is this not a good way to show the audience our fisherman's life?"

Sol grunted, "Here we go again, Mort, you keep adding to the film; the scriptwriters are going to love this!"

As the door closed behind them, Belle looked at everyone and said, "I will not be joining you all for dinner tonight; I have a date."

Blaine grinned at Cecile and Farron, "I guess we know who the lucky man is."

"Who?" Farron asked.

Belle smiled, "With a very handsome man, the one who connected my phones. He is a Frenchman, born in the United States; he likes me and has asked me to dine with him at a steak house in Newport Beach."

Chuckling, Farron tried not to look amused, "Sounds as if you have found a reason for living?"

Mary entered just in time to hear the friendly bantering between Farron and Belle, "Now stop that, Farron. You should be happy for Belle. I'm thrilled to see she has more to do here than work. He is a hunk! He looks like a movie star. Way to go, girl! How lucky can you get, and a Frenchman!"

Farron kissed Mary, "You are not supposed to notice other men; remember, you are going to be a mother, and you can only have eyes for the baby's daddy."

"I have eyes for no other, and you know it. However, I am not blind, and that man is good-looking. What's his name?"

Dancing around in a little circle, Belle picked up the coffee pot and filled her cup, "His name is Philip Dubois; he was born in Louisiana. Is that a nice state? How far is it from California?"

Blaine thought for a couple of minutes, "Let's see, from here you go through Arizona, New Mexico, Texas, and finally come to Louisiana; I would guess it must be close to two thousand miles. Did he say what part? It's a beautiful state, but humid because they get lots of rain, and it's near the Gulf of Mexico and the Mississippi River, also, if he is from New Orleans, Lake Ponchartrain. New Orleans is French, and the heart of the city is called the French Quarter. Fabulous Restaurants and French cuisine."

Cecile pushed a freshly baked croissant in front of Blaine, "And how do you know so much about New Orleans?"

Cecile, my dear, "I think you forgot, when your old man was young, he worked on an offshore oil rig in the Gulf of Mexico, close to New Orleans, visited the French Quarter and saw shows on Bourbon Street. Working on the oil rig was dangerous, and at that time, my living quarters on top of the rig was small. There came a hurricane, and it scared the hell out of me, so I quit and returned to Indiana, the farm, and the world I knew. When we met, I had just begun to make money with my grain elevator. We fell in love, got married, you had our baby, Farron, and shortly after became very ill with Asthma. The doctor said to leave the area because the weather and moisture would kill you, so here we are, and the rest is history."

Tears fell from Cecile's eyes; she went to Blaine and kissed him. "Yes, I remember everything. It was a struggle, but we made it, and here you are a stone-throw from the ocean and can fish as much as you like."

'Yes," Blaine returned, "and it's easier than fishing from the bottom of an oil rig or slapping mosquitos on a lake in Indiana. We are not rich, Cecile, but we have it all, you have your health, we make a living, we have friends, and we have Farron and Mary. What more could a man asked."

Cecile kissed Blaine again, "Nothing, dear, we have it all." She turned, rushed into the hallway, and began to cough.

Mary saw and followed, "What is it, Cecile? What's wrong?"

While struggling to catch her breath, Cecile held up one hand and motioned for Mary to hush, "I don't want Blaine to see me coughing. Lately, I have these spells too often. At night I sneak out of bed and go into the bathroom and flush the toilet so that Blaine won't hear me."

Mary shook her head, "Cecile, you must not keep this from Blaine. Something can be done for you; this is not the old days. For instance, you could get relief from this attack by using an inhaler. Have you seen a doctor? If not, you must tell Blaine that you are not well. You might be allergic to cooking, with certain vegetables, or fruit, or all the smoke that comes from things frying."

"I know, Mary, and I promise that I will see a doctor, but not before Blaine goes on the fishing trip with Farron. Blaine believes that the fresh air from the sea has cured me, but there is no cure for asthma. Were I to tell him now, he would not go on the trip. And Mary, he needs that trip; he is a ham actor and wants the camera on him.

Farron hates the idea of acting; he is a fisherman, but his father would love to be in a movie." Cecile coughed a little and continued, "Mary, I love my husband the way you love Farron, and did you tell Farron you were pregnant when he went to Alaska? No, you did not; and for the same reason, I will wait to tell Blaine about my asthma attacks. If he were to see me with an inhaler, he would know something is wrong. I can't do that to him, Mary, please understand."

Chapter 9

Farron stood on the flying deck of his thirty-three foot Sport Fisher seacraft and waved at Belle as he pulled away from the dock, and Belle, thankful for remaining on shore, turned to Philip and teased, "Now, we can play, n'est ce pas?"

"I made reservations for us tonight, at eight, at The Shanghai Pine Garden Restaurant. So get your sweet little self ready for a treat."

"Being with you is a treat. I was supposed to leave the harbor with Farron and the film crew, but thankfully, the producer changed his mind. They are going fishing for Bluefin Tuna, and from what they told me, I want no part of it. They are going far south, maybe as far as the Mexican border."

"Wow! Bluefin Tuna fishing sounds exciting! I would like to do that one day but hardly have the time. My weekends come and go too quickly. Of course, I could take a week off and fish with your friend, Farron." Philip looked up at the sky and gazed out to sea, "By the looks of the sky, Farron could be in for a little bad weather. This is the monsoon time of year, and anything can happen. I am glad they didn't take you; I can't picture you with a fishing rod in your hand."

"Never!" Belle returned, "I will never kill a fish or anything! I hate to think about it, and I hate to think that something must die for us to eat."

"Do you not want to go to dinner?"

"Philip, of course, I want to go to dinner; it's just that for the first time in my life, I think about what I eat. My mother would think nothing of wringing a chicken's neck or boiling a crab, but since Farron told me how they kill a giant fish, all those things come to mind."

Philip began to laugh, "Well, I am taking you to dinner at the Shanghai Pine Garden restaurant, and I certainly hope you will eat! Do you like pork? If so, they serve great sweet and sour pork? However, if you choose, they also serve soups, salads, and vegetarian dishes."

"I don't care, Philip, as long as I am with you, I'm sure everything will be wonderful. I will be ready and waiting by seven-thirty."

Unfortunately, Philip was right about the weather, and when they reached the restaurant, the rain was bucketing down. He stopped by the front door, "You run on in and get seated, just tell them you have a reservation and give them my name; I will park the car and be right there."

Belle covered her head with a newspaper, ran for the front door, entered, and was seated quickly. Moments later, Philip came through the door, dripping wet, and was directed to their table. The waiter held Philip's chair, took his coat, and said, "This will dry while you are eating. We could have sent someone with an umbrella for you."

"Thank you. My suit is dry, and I am fine." He looked at Belle, "Darn, it would rain! We have a perfect table, and if it were not for the rain, we could see the Pacific Ocean."

"The rain is all the water we need, Philip; just think about Farron out there on the sea, and I could have been with him."

"I am afraid they are in for a blow, but I'm sure it is not a first for Farron," Philip returned.

Belle closed her eyes and shook her head as the memory of Bill drowning during the storm in Alaska returned; she grew pale and trembled. Philip reached across the table and held her hand, "What is it, Belle? You are trembling."

"I need a drink," she said, "something strong."

Philip motioned for the waiter, "Do you serve Scotch?"

"Oh yes, we have the finest, Suntory Royal, made in the Orient."

"Bring a bottle and two glasses with ice."

The waiter left returned with the glasses and Scotch, poured each a drink, and Philip waved him away. "Belle, dear, I know the memory of another storm is haunting you, and I wish I could make you forget, but who am I? Someone who works for the telephone company, someone who loves you."

Belle reached for her glass and sipped the scotch. "I am so sorry, Philip; I don't want to ruin our evening. Since you and I met, I seldom think of Bill, but the storm, and the thought of Farron out there in this weather, brings back the memory of Bill going down with his ship, and the baby I lost. I am so thankful for you; you have changed my life, and I must not allow the past to take our happiness away." She held his hand to her lips, kissed it, and released it, saying, "and thank you for understanding. Now let us order, and worry no more about Farron out there fighting the weather. He knows the sea, and he will be safe." She glanced out at the rain, "I am happy to be here and not out there with him."

"I think the entire thing is insane," Philip returned, "I'm sure the studios have miles of stock film with boats fishing the Pacific Ocean in storms, and they could always dub-in shots of Farron at the helm."

"I feel the same, but of course, it would not be the same kind of sea craft as Farron's."

Philip laughed, "I hardly think that would be noticed in a storm, but Hollywood does things their way, and who am I to say?"

Belle glanced at the menu, sighed, and said, "Why don't we have the Family Dinner; it comes with Wonton soup, Egg-rolls, Paper wrapped chicken, Cream cheese Wonton, Kun Pao Chicken, and rice.."

Philip grinned, "That sounds good to me, but I will order an extra entre of Sweet and Sour Pork; it's my favorite."

Looking at Philip with loved filled eyes, Belle murmured,

"This is much better than going fishing."

Belle was right because, at that moment, Farron was fighting the sea and ordered Blaine, "Put on your lifejacket and get below with the rest of the men. We're in trouble! I'm heading for Dana Point Harbor."

"No," Blaine shouted, "I'll stay with you!"

"Dad!" Farron raised his voice, "Don't argue! Do as I say, and now!"

Grumbling, Blaine strumbled down the steps and pushed up next to a cameraman."I hope you guys are satisfied, we got that damn fish, and now with luck, we will get to shore with it!"

The cameraman sitting next to him replied, "If I live through this, I'm going to quit my job. From the start, this whole damn thing has been a nightmare, first fighting to catch that big ugly Bluefin, then cleaning it, and storing it. And, it's not going to mean shit if we sink!" He glared at Blaine, "For Christ's sake, fasten your lifejacket, man! If this thing goes down, you don't want to go with it, do you?"

"We won't go down," Blaine answered, "my boy knows what he's doing, and he'll get us in safely. We are almost to Dana Point, and will soon be inside the harbor."

At Dana Point, they neared the breakwater with a following sea, their small craft pushed forward, and Farron picked up speed to keep from getting swamped. The boat turned toward one side of the harbor, and back, as Farron struggled to stay ahead of the sea. Crossing himself, he prayed, "Lord give us a few more yards past the breakwater, and we'll be all right." In answer to his prayer, the water began to calm; Farron breathed a huge sigh and slowed the boat. "We're in, thank you, God," and he shouted, "how are you guys doing down there?"

A loud moan came from below, and Blaine answered, "We are alive, but barely, and our stomachs are not too happy. Is it safe to come up?"

Farron answered, "Yes, come on up. I see the Harbor Police headed for us, and if you with the camera can stand on your feet, you should come up and film it. The police will have us follow them, and they will find us a slip." He came to a stop and waited for the Harbor patrol to come alongside.

One of the officers asked, "What in the hell were you doing with this toy-boat out there in this storm?"

"Fishing," Farron replied.

"You must be nuts," the officer replied and glared at the man holding the camera. "What were you doing? Were you taking pictures of a storm?"

"If I didn't need the money," the cameraman replied, "I would not be here. This trip was my first and last at sea, from now on its terra-firma. I'm filming no more movies on a boat."

"You risk your lives to make a movie? Who's the star, and what's the name of the movie?"

"Unfortunately," Farron replied, "I am the so-called star. The movie began in Alaska, fishing the Bering Straits; we were in a storm, the boat went down, and I survived, now, Hollywood wants to complete the movie." He chuckled, "It damn near got finished today! I don't know what they intend to call it, and I don't give a damn. To hell with acting!"

The officer directed them into a slip and handed Farron a card, "If the movie ever gets made, let me know. For now, you should stay put until this bad weather ends. If you want to use our facilities," he pointed toward a row of buildings, "you will find showers and things up there. Just sign these papers, and let me see your license." He handed Farron a piece of paper, "This is your permit to stay in the harbor until the storm ends." He tipped his hat and pulled away.

Everyone got out of the boat and ran for the showers while Farron called home. Cecile answered, "Oh My God!" she exclaimed. "We have been worried to death! We watched the news and saw people getting off of a sinking boat just outside the harbor. It was about the same size as yours, and all we could do was pray and wait to hear from you. How is Blaine? Is he all right?"

"Yes, mom, we are all doing fine. Dad is a trooper and had no fear. We caught a Bluefin; it will be in the movie, and so will dad. I'll tell you all about it when we get home. How is my little Mary?"

Cecile handed the phone to Mary, and Mary crying said,

"Farron, darling, thank God you are alive. I have been so afraid for you! Where are you, and when will you be home? I could have miscarried waiting for this call."

Farron choked out, "I'm sorry, darling, but we were in some very high seas, and I could not reach you. We are in the harbor at Dana Point and will be here tonight and maybe tomorrow. We are tired but safe. The boat is tied up in a slip, and we are walking distance to a harbor restaurant. Everyone else is taking a shower in the harbor facilities, after which we will go for food, and then rest. Please take care of yourself, and don't climb any stairs." He made a sound like a kiss, "I love you. Don't ask me any more questions because I am anxious to shower, eat, and sleep."

"Okay, dear," Mary replied, "You don't know how much I love you; if I had lost you in this storm, the baby and I would be lost. Now, tonight I will also sleep." She hung up the phone and turned to find Cecile, coughing uncontrollably. Excited, she pushed Cecile into a chair and rushed to get her a glass of water. "Here," she said, "try to take a swallow of this, it might help. These attacks are happening too often?"

Cecile sipped the water and tried to catch her breath. "Mary, you didn't see this; please say nothing. I thank the Lord that Blaine was not here to see this spell; he would want to rush me off to a doctor."

"Of course he would," Mary returned, "and tomorrow, you will see a doctor. You can no longer keep this from your husband. Blaine loves you, Cecile. He brought you to California to keep you alive, but since then, things have changed, and you need help."

"I know, Mary. One of these days I will die coughing."

Belle, entering from her evening with Philip, saw Cecile, coughing and gasping for air, and alarmed, she asked, "My God! What's wrong?"

"Cecile is having an asthma attack; help me get her to bed. This rain, the damp air, and hearing from Farron brought this on. She will be all right in a few minutes. They each held on to Cecile while they got her into the bedroom and in bed. "Should I open a window?" Belle asked.

"No, no, Belle," Mary answered, "the moisture would make it worse. We will wait here with her until she starts to breathe normally, and then I will call a doctor. She doesn't want a doctor, but she's going to have one. And while we're waiting, there is a letter for you from France on the office desk."

"From France," Belle squealed and ran for office. "It must be from my mother! Oh, I hope it is! I hope she is on her way to America!" She picked up the letter, ripped it open and read: It was difficult for me to get ready; I had much to do and so many friends and goodbyes. I will leave Paris the day after tomorrow, Wednesday, from Charles de Gaulle airport at 9:19 pm our time, and arrive at the Los Angeles airport at 6:04 am your time. Please be waiting because I am so excited and nervous." Belle ran with the news to Mary and Cecile, "My mother arrives Wednesday.

Oh, I can hardly wait!"

"Quiet," Mary warned, "Cecile is sleeping, and the doctor is on his way. I know you are excited, Belle, and I am happy for you, but so much is happening, I feel as if I could faint. We know that Farron and Blaine are safe, and you have your wonderful news, but I am anxious about Cecile and fear she could die before either of the men get home." Mary began to cry, "I don't know what to do! I'm so upset and afraid."

"You must calm yourself, Mary; Cecile is not going to die, and the doctor will be here shortly. You must quiet yourself!" She stopped and listened, "There, the doorbell, the doctor. Go to the door and let him in."

Mary opened the door, and a tall elderly man with gray hair introduced himself, "I am Doctor McFinney if you will show me to the patient."

Mary quickly took him into Cecile's bedroom, where they found Cecile gasping for air. Immediately using a medicated inhaler, the doctor placed it under Cecile's nose and told her to breathe as deeply as possible. She did so and, in a matter of seconds, began to breathe normally. "My dear," McFinney said, "you are lucky someone was here to help you. I am going to leave this inhaler with you and the medication to go with it; I want to see you in my office tomorrow. You are a very sick lady! We must do something about this before it is too late."

Wide-eyed, Cecile said, "It will be difficult. I don't want my

husband to know about this."

The doctor laughed, "If you don't tell him, I will. Now, something brought this on. Have you been nervous and upset about something?"

Mary interrupted, "Yes, we have all be nervous and upset, our husbands have been at sea in this storm. We are alright now because we received news that they are in port at Dana Point. Cecile's asthma attack happened when we heard they were safe."

The doctor thanked Mary and reminded her to get Cecile into his office, and of course, she promised. The door closed behind him, and she said, "Belle, if I were not pregnant, I would have a big slug of whiskey."

"I'll get you some hot chocolate," Belle returned, "maybe that will help," and they both laughed. "You must be well when my mother arrives; she might be here before Farron gets home. I will pick her up at the airport, a new experience for me, driving in this country, and this city!"

Fearful of the traffic, Belle left early and waited an hour for the plane from France to land. As she saw her mother, she ran to her, kissed her, and during a wild exchange of words in French, rushed her to the luggage department. Once in the car and headed for the beach, Belle reminded her mother that she must speak English while in the presence of others because no one in the family spoke or understood French. "I will introduce you as

Juliette, I don't think they should call you mere', mother."

They both laughed, and as Belle neared the boarding house, she pointed, "That's it; that's where we live. You might have thought I would live in Hollywood, and in time we will, but for now, we are lucky to have this."

Juliette looked up and noticed the plants hanging from one of the balconies, "That must be your apartment," she said and laughed. "This is not a bad looking building, it just needs new paint, and more flowers hanging from balconies; the way we do it in Paris."

Belle parked behind the building and directed her mother to the back door. "Why are we entering from the back of the building?"

"Because this is where we park. We will enter through the kitchen, and I expect most of the family will be there having coffee and talking about my co-star's recent experience while fishing to complete the film." She rolled her eyes, "We will talk about it later."

Disappointed, they found no one but Mary in the kitchen, and Mary greeted Belle's mother with a smile, a hug, and asked if the trip was pleasant. "We expect the men soon. They would be here by now, but because of the storm, they were delayed and spent the night at Dana Point." As she spoke, the door opened, and the men entered. Farron whisked Mary up into his arms and kissed her. Cecile entered the room looking pale, saw

Blaine, and ran to him. "Thank the Lord, at last, you are home!" she exclaimed as Blaine lifted her off the floor and kissed her.

 "Now, my love," Blaine said, "get me a huge cup of coffee and a stack of pancakes smothered in syrup." He sat at the table, spread the newspaper on the table, and waited. Belle stepped in front of him, and Blaine looked up. "Can I do something for you, Belle?"

"Are you too tired to see," Belle asked? "Did you notice nothing when you entered? Look, my mother is here, and I want you to meet her, Juliette Fauche'. She just arrived from Paris."

He pushed the paper aside and stood up to face Belle's mother; at the same time, Juliette, a ravishingly beautiful, dark-haired beauty, extended her hand, "It is my pleasure to meet such a handsome man."

Cecile eyed Juliette and glared at Blaine as he openly admired Belle's mother, took her hand in his, held it, and in French, returned her greeting, "Mon Plaisir Madame Fauche', et tu es Presque aussi belle que ma femme." He sent a smile to Cecile.

Juliette quickly retrieved her hand and blushed, "Excusez moi," she replied, turned to look at Cecile and in English said, "You are this handsome man's wife; I am so happy to meet you."

Looking confused and amused, Cecile answered, "Please excuse the way I look; I did not sleep well. My husband is having breakfast, but I must prepare lunch for our other guests. I hope you will join us. We serve all meals in the dining room. May I get you a cup of coffee or tea? I know you must be tired from your trip."

"Thank you; I think not; Belle is anxious for me to see her apartment." She glanced at Belle, thanked Cecile, and nodded for Belle to lead the way.

Cecile glared at Blaine, "And what was all that? I didn't know you could speak French!"

Blaine laughed, "There is always room for a little humor in life, my sweet, beautiful little wife. The lady was out of line; I put her in her place and let her know that I have a wife as beautiful as she." He laughed, "She is a bit fresh, but I suppose that's the French way? I was stationed just outside of Paris during the war, and learning a little of the language was necessary."

Cecile joined in with the laughter, "If I live to be a hundred, I will never know all there is to know about you."

Blaine went to Cecile, put his arms around her, and kissed her. "We have been through a lot together, and we've weathered the storms. I nearly lost you in Indiana; now we are here, you are well, and our lives are complete. You are my woman, and you are all I need or want. I love you."

Knowing she was not well, Cecile trembled, wiped tears out of her eyes, and replied, "I love you with all my heart, Blaine, and when a beautiful woman tells you how handsome you are, I see red!"

"That's my girl," Blaine held her tightly, "have no fear, no one can ever take your place."

Cecile clung to him and thought, not while I'm alive. "I should finish with these meals, Blaine, but I am tired from too much worry." She looked at Mary and asked, "Mary, could you take over for me, you and Farron. The menus are on the counter, and you know where everything is. When Blaine finishes eating his breakfast, we will go to the room; I need an extra nap.

Blaine wiped his lips with his napkin, rose from the table, and said, "Sounds good to me! Come on, dear; I want to hold you in my arms."

As they left the room, Farron looked at Mary, "Would you care to tell me what's going on? Mom never walks away from her cooking."

Holding back tears, Mary sat across the table from Farron and confessed. "I promised Cecile I would not tell, but you must know, and so must Blaine. Your mother is very ill. Her asthma has worsened, and she has trouble breathing. I am to take her to the doctor tomorrow.

"No!" Farron exclaimed, "I thought the salt air had cured her."

"There is no cure for asthma, Farron. Your mother has been keeping the way she feels away from us, but today she had an attack, and I thought she was going to die. She works too hard in this place; I must do more for her. Bell said her mother is a cook,

maybe she will help? I will ask later; it's too soon now. But for now, you can help me; come and look at this menu and start cleaning vegetables while I prepare tonight's roast beef." Farron turned in circles, looked confused, and Mary kept giving orders. "For lunch, the guests will get a bowl of chili and beans, some warm tortillas, and a salad. There's beer in the frigidaire, for the men who want it, and there's a pitcher of lemonade, plus cokes for the others. Some may prefer sandwiches, and we have sliced ham, tomatoes, lettuce, and all the trimmings. It will be up to you to ask each person his preference. If they want sandwiches, we will put everything, including condiments, in the center of each table, and they can all make there own. Oh, and we have a bowl of potato salad in the fridge, we will include that."

"Jesus!" Farron uttered, "Does mom do all this every day?"

"Yes, honey, she does this and more, has done for years, and it has caught up with her. She is not young, and she is not well, and can no longer do all this work. I pray Belle's mother will help; if not, we must find someone who can."

Noises began to come from the dining room, and Mary glanced at Farron, "Here we go, honey, we're on. I know you are tired, and you smell like a fish, so rush into the showers, and I'll get things started."

On his way to the shower, Farron met his father on the stairs, "Got to clean up and take care of our guests; why don't you do the same?"

"Okay, I'll be right with you, but first, I want to talk to Mary; Cecile is acting strange."

"She's pretty busy, dad; you should wait until the guests are taken care of and then talk to her. Her hands are full right now. Mary is used to serving but not cooking. Hop in the shower with me, and then you can help us."

Blaine followed Farron into the shower, and while the water was running down their bodies, he asked, "Farron, do you know what is wrong with your mother?"

Farron stepped out of the shower, dried off, and slipped into his clothes, "Yes, dad, I do. Mom is not well; her asthma has worsened. She had an attack today, and Mary called a doctor."

"That's not possible," Blaine returned, "I brought her here to get her well, and she is well!"

"No, dad, she is not. There is no cure for asthma. She begged Mary not to tell you, but you must know. Right now, she is using an inhaler with some sort of medication in it, and it helps her to breathe. We don't know what else the doctor can do for her, and Mary is taking her to see him tomorrow. Is mom resting now?"

"Yes, she was asleep when I left the room."

"Then get a move on; we have guests to wait-on."

They entered the kitchen at the same time as Belle and Juliette, and Juliette looked around, "My word, I thought your

mother did all this; where is she?"

"My wife," Blaine answered, "is very ill and can no longer do all these things. Farron and Mary have taken over for now, but we don't know what we are going to do. Mary is not a cook; at least she doesn't know how to cook for so many people. Most of our guests have all their meals with us, breakfast, lunch, and dinner, which means up in the mornings early, in time to serve breakfast. They take what we serve for all meals; we do not have a menu."

"I am sorry to hear that your wife is ill; perhaps I can help; I am a professional cook; there is nothing I cannot make. Belle told me that you refuse to allow her to pay rent, and for that, I can be your cook."

Blaine went to Juliette, framed her face with his hands, and kissed her forehead, "Bless you. God must have sent you to us."

Juliette felt a surge of excitement rush through her as his lips touched her face, and wide-eyed, she looked up into his eyes, and said, "I am happy to help."

Chapter 10

Two months later, Belle and Farron were paid in full for their appearances in "No Time To Lose," and received word that they and company could view the film the evening of the sixteenth at Upton Studios. It was nearing time for Mary to deliver. She leaned back in her chair and stared at Farron, "Do you think I should go, Farron? Look at the size of my belly; it could be any time now, and I wouldn't want to deliver our baby in between the seats of a theatre."

Farron laughed, "I would not like that either. My sweet wife, if you are afraid, don't go; you can see the film any other time. The scenes in Alaska might cause you to deliver. To tell you the truth, I am worried about Belle; while filming, she lost her love, Captain Bill Armstrong."

"She will go," Mary replied, "accompanied by Philip, and lean on his big broad shoulder."

"Yes, a voice from the doorway said, "Of course, we will all go, Philip, my mother, and me. Juliette will love it; she has never seen me on the screen. Now that you know her, you know she is ready for anything."

Cecile smiled quietly to herself, thinking Juliette was ready for too much, including Blaine. "Yes," Cecile, responded, "your mother is quite a woman; it's as if she is heaven-sent. She turned and eyed Blaine, who was busy reading the news and heard not a word.

"I came to borrow a few cubes of sugar, may I? We're having tea on the balcony with Philip; Juliette adores him."

"Take whatever you need," Cecile replied, waited, and as Belle left and the door closed behind her, she turned to Farron, "Now listen, the night of the filming, when we are seated in the theatre, you make sure that you sit on one side of Blaine and I will sit on the other. I don't want that woman rubbing shoulders with Blaine. I know she is a good person, but she has eyes for your father."

Blaine heard, looked up, and laughed, "My sweet wife, how many times have I told you that there would never be anyone for me but you. Come here and kiss your old man."

Farron chuckled, "I'll keep an eye on him for you, mom."

Cecile kissed Blaine, "I do appreciate how she has taken over in the kitchen, and she is a fabulous cook; she has made life much easier for me. Is she doing it for me, or is she doing it to make an impression on you, Blaine?"

Blaine pulled Cecile down on his lap, "She is doing it for you, Cecile, and in doing so, she is also doing it for me. You know how much I love you, and I could not live without you. You are my life, now and forever."

"And you are mine," Cecile whispered.

Mary began to laugh, "You two are like a couple of kids," she said, and suddenly stopped, bent forward, and moaned, "Oh, oh, Farron, I think you had better get me to the hospital; beneath

her was a puddle of water. I'm ready to deliver."

"Oh, my God!" Farron shouted, "Mom, what shall I do?"

Cecile smiled, "Calm down, get Mary into the car and get her to the hospital. Blaine will go with you. Now each of you help her into the car and call me as soon as she is settled. I will call the hospital and let them know you are coming, and her doctor will be there. Don't drive too fast because there is time; it will take a while for the baby to come."

Despite Cecile's warning, Farron raced through the traffic, blowing his horn, and reached the hospital within twenty minutes. Once there, a nurse took Mary to a room by herself, and the doctor told Farron and Blaine, "You might have a long wait; we never know. It could take as long as twenty-four hours for Mary to deliver. The baby does not come right after the water breaks; on the other hand, she could deliver sooner. Have some coffee and relax."

"Can I be in the room with my wife," Farron asked.

"Yes," doctor St. James replied, "you can stay with her through the delivery."

Farron handed the car keys to Blaine, "You go home, dad, and I'll call you when it's over."

Blaine happily took the keys, "Mary will be fine," he said and left; he'd been through this when Farron was born and knew what Farron was mentally going through.

Farron went into the room with Mary and sat in a chair beside her bed, "You don't need to be here," she said, "you can't have the baby for me."

"I am here, and here I stay. I am going to be here when our baby pops out."

Mary laughed, "I wish it were as easy as that! It can't just pop out! When the baby is ready, it will cause me pain, and you will get upset because I must help it come. So, behave yourself because if you don't, the doctor will put you out of the room."

Time went by slowly, and Farron fell asleep in the chair beside Mary's bed, but about eight hours later, he awoke when she screamed; the baby was trying to come. Nurses entered the room, and Mary gripped the sides of the bed; "It's coming," she said, "help me." Her forehead was wet with sweat, and her cheeks were flushed, "Oh God," she screamed, "Oh God, help me!"

The doctor entered, examined her, and said, "Your Cervix is open, and the baby is trying to come out. It is sooner than I expected. He remained at the foot of the bed, "Every time you feel pain and have the urge to push, push. You're doing fine; your cervix is all the way open now, but this will take a while." Ten hours later, the struggle ended, and Mary gave birth to a baby boy. Through sweat and tears, she squeezed Farron's hand, "We did it," she cried,

"I couldn't have done it without you here for me." A nurse put the baby in Mary's arms, and she continued to cry, "We will call him John, after his great grandfather. That will

please Blaine and Cecile. Do you agree?"

Farron kissed Mary, and gingerly touched the baby, "Yes, I think that's a grand idea."

Mary held a shaky hand up to Farron's face, "I think you should go home now and rest; you've had a hard night."

"Yes, we've had a hard night. I love you, Mary, and when you were going through so much pain, I prayed to God that you would live. I was so afraid I was going to lose you. I would die without you, Mary, and on the way out, I will stop in the Chapel and give our thanks to God."

Three days later, Mary and the baby left the hospital, went home, and into the bedroom next to Cecile's and Blaine's. Beside the bed, connected between two stanchions, was a cradle. "What's this?" Mary asked.

Farron grinned, took the baby out of her arms, and placed it in the cradle. "This was my cradle, one that dad made. When the baby cries, you can rock it without getting out of bed, like this." He rocked the cradle.

Mary climbed into bed, "give me the baby; right now, I want him beside me. He might get hungry."

Everyone entered the room to peek at the baby, and eyes filled with tears, Cecile leaned over, kissed him, and said, "He looks just like his father, Farron. He will grow up and be a fisherman." She then reached for a chair and sat beside the bed. "I'll rest here a while with you; I know you are tired."

Not noticing, Blaine patted Farron on the back, "You did good, son," he said, "make the next one a girl."

Cecile began to cough, and Blaine went to her, "Blaine, I can't breathe," she took the inhaler from her pocket, "help me."

Juliette went to Cecile, "Blaine, help me get your wife to bed. She's had too much excitement; come."

Blaine gently lifted Cecile out of her chair and carried her into the next bedroom. Juliette pulled back the covers and carefully removed Cecile's clothes, slipped a loose nightgown on her, propped pillows behind her head, and said,

"Now, Cecile, breathe in deeply with your inhaler, until you feel better. Blaine, you stay with your wife while I get her some hot green tea. It will help relax the muscles in her lungs, like a bronchodilator and open up her airways. I will be quick," she rushed from the room, and minutes later returned with the tea. "Now, Blaine," she ordered, "help Cecile sit up while I get her to sip on this tea."

Speechless, Blaine followed Juliette's orders, sat on the bed next to Cecile, and held her up as Juliette held a cup to her mouth, saying, "Drink. I know it's not easy, but you must drink."

Cecile tried to smile, and tears were in her eyes. "Do not cry," Juliette ordered, "you will make it harder to breathe. Sip on this tea while it is hot."

Cecile did as ordered, and after a few sips of the hot tea, she began to breathe a little easier."

Blaine eased Cecile back on the pillows and looked at

Juliette, in amazement, "Where and how did you learn all this?"

"My late husband suffered from Asthma and struggled with it for many years."

"And did he die from it?" Blaine asked.

"No, he did not. He died from kidney failure, but I do not wish to remember or talk about the loss of my beloved husband. Cecile is not going to die, but she will have other days like this. I think that's why God sent Belle here to live with you so that she would send for me, and I could be here to help Cecile. We all have a purpose on this earth; we may not know what it is, but the good Lord directs our paths."

Cecile, now breathing easily, reached for Juliette's hand, "God bless you; I am so thankful for all you do." She smiled, "When I first saw you, I was jealous because you are so beautiful, and you admired my husband; forgive me. I am no longer jealous; bless you."

Juliette looked at Blaine, "Stay here, and I will bring more hot tea. Can I also bring you something?"

"Yes, please bring and extra cup and a croissant; all this excitement has made me hungry." Blaine looked at Cecile, "Would you also like a croissant?"

"Have you made cookies," Cecile asked? If so, I might be able to dunk one in my tea and get it down."

Juliette left the room and peeked in on Mary, the baby, and

Farron. "I'm on my way to the kitchen, is there anything I can bring you?"

Bleary-eyed from fatigue, Farron said, "Mary and the baby are sleeping; I will follow you into the kitchen, and if you get a chance, I would love some bacon and eggs."

"Of course, Belle is serving the guests in the dining room; why don't you join them, and she will give you whatever you like."

Farron stopped just inside the dining room door as Mort and Sol grinned and said, "We thought you would never get here. We heard about the baby, went to the hospital, and they told us that you and the wife had left. Belle met us at the door and asked if we would like to have breakfast. Would we say no? You know us; we're always ready for food. You all missed the filming, and we were worried because we knew Belle wanted to see herself on the screen." They laughed, "We will have a private screening again, just for you."

Farron sat on a chair across from Mort, "That's very nice of you. I am in luck; everything is going my way. We finished filming, and I am the father of a six-pound boy named John."

"You did a great job, and it has paid off; the studios are crazy about you and want us to sign you up." Mort pushed a contract toward Farron. "The way you caught the Bluefin Tuna, cleaned it and stored it in the middle of a storm, was fantastic, and we think your dad will like the way he looked in the film too."

Farron smiled, "I love you guys, I really do, and I appreciate this offer, but I cannot accept it."

"Don't be a fool, Farron, listen to what we have to offer before you say no. This contract is not for a movie; it is for a television series about you and the sea. If it hits, it could go on forever, and you will be rolling in money."

"It sounds great, but no. Again, I must tell you; I am not an actor; I am a fisherman, and I am happy with the money I make chartering fishing trips with men who want to catch a few Bass to take home to their wives."

Mort insisted, "So! You see, that would be great in a fishing series on television."

"You cannot fool me, Mort, not this time. I know it would call for scripts with excitement, possibly tragedies, and love affairs, and you would want Belle in it. No way! I am through with the camera and your movie ideas. Get someone else, and allow me my kind of life without interruption. I have a wife and a son, and I will go on making less money my way."

Mort and Sol would not give it up. "Think it over; take this contract and look it over, and you might change your mind."

"Can I get you something, Farron," Belle asked, and looked at Mort, "you see, If I don't don't get me a part in a movie, I can always be a waitress."

Sol and Mort laughed, "You? Never! You love acting, and

will never do anything else. We're trying to talk this guy into doing a television series, and he refuses."

Excited, Belle looked at Farron, "Are you crazy! Why don't you accept their offer? Think of all the money you would make in a series on television! And, maybe if you agree, I can have a part in it!"

"Listen to me, Belle, I know you want to act, and you can; push Mort a little, and I'm sure he will get you a film, but I am not like you; I was not born with a desire to act. I want peace of mind and a family. I do not want to get in front of a camera, not for any amount of money."

"This man is out of his mind," Belle grumbled, "and he doesn't care about me! If he did a series for you, I could be in it! He is selfish," she pouted. "Now, when will we get to see our Alaskan adventure? At least, allow me that!"

Sol answered, "Give us a couple more weeks, and we'll arrange another private viewing. We will call you, don't you call us!" Mort and Sol snickered, "That's a stock joke!"

Belle frowned and shrugged her shoulders, "I don't understand; I would not call you unless I get married and quit acting!"

Surprised, Mort asked, "Belle, have you met someone who has stolen your heart?"

"Yes, I have, and he is very handsome; he could be a movie

star; he looks like Louis Jourdan."

Each could see where she was going, and Belle blushed. "I am not trying to get him into acting! I just wanted you to know that I will not die if I never make another movie!" She turned and poured coffee into each cup.

Changing the subject, Farron asked, "Would you like to see my son? I am very proud of him. He is probably in the kitchen with Mary. She is trying to help mom and Juliette do things, and has the baby in a crib near her.

"Juliette," Mort and Sol looked up, "who is Juliette?"

"Juliette is my beautiful mother," Belle said, "who is here from France. She is living with me, and she speaks very little English; would you like to meet her?"

Mort replied, "Yes, of course; please bring her in."

Belle left and returned with her mother and introduced her to Mort and Sol. Mort stood up and took her hand, "I am pleased to meet you, and I must say you are as beautiful as your daughter."

"Je vous remercie. C'est une exage'ration, mais accepte'e."

"What did she say," both Mort and Sol asked?

"She said that you compliment her and exaggerate, but she accepts your compliment. She will also accept a part in films."

Juliette replied in English, "My daughter's words!"

Chapter 11

"My dear little wife," Farron pulled Mary down on his lap, "those Hollywood moguls were here again trying to interest me into taking another job making movies; but, this time it was for a television series. I refused because I do not want to take time away from my family. Of course, their offer included a large amount of money, but I told them I was satisfied with the money I make chartering bass-fishing trips."

"Good, you refused," Mary answered, "I don't want you mixing in with all those Hollywood people. They are not like us; we are simple people, and we don't drink, throw wild parties, or sleep with other's husbands or wives. I know they are not all like that, but from what I see on the news, it is pretty wild. Do they honestly want you for a television series?" She stopped talking and carefully considered the offer, "Of course, the money would be nice; we could put it away for John's future."

"Stop, Mary," John can make his own future, just as I have. We want for nothing; I like our life, and I love living with the family and all our boarding house friends. What could Hollywood give us that we don't have here? The nearness of family and good friends, good health, a roof over our heads, and plenty to eat is all we need in this world. Money does not bring happiness; as a matter of fact, it often brings misery. As the apostle Paul said, money is the root of all evil. He didn't exactly say it that way, but that's what it meant."

Mary touched Farron's cheek and kissed him, "I love you so

much; you are a good man, and you are right. We have everything we need and more; we are blessed. You do as you like, charter fishing trips, and don't go out in bad weather. Stay close to home, so if there is a need, I can get you on the ship-to-shore phone. I prefer to live without the fear of losing you at sea.

A scream came from the hallway, and Belle rushed in, "It's Cecile! She is on the floor at the foot of the stairs; come!"

When they reached Cecile, they found Juliette on the floor with Cecile's head on her lap, holding an inhaler under her nose. "Go quickly, bring hot tea," she said, "and call an ambulance."

Farron fell on his knees beside her, "Someone get dad, please."

Within seconds, Blaine was on the floor next to Cecile, pleading with her to live. "Cecile," he begged, "please breathe, don't die; please don't die."

The hot tea came, Mary shakily handed a cup to Juliette, and Juliette lifted Cecile's head enough to allow her to sip the tea. "There now," she said, "let it go down slowly to open up those airways." Cecile's eyes rolled back in her head, and she tried to open them, "You will be all right," Juliette said, "just try to sip the tea. She tilted the cup but got no response. "S'il te plait Dieu ne la prends pas," she begged God, "do not take her."

Paramedics arrived, checked Cecile, and rushed her into the ambulance. Blaine followed, sat beside her, and Farron, holding one of Cecile's hands, knelt next to Blaine.

"Cecile don't leave me; please, don't leave me," Blaine begged. Cecile's fingers moved, and her lips formed, I love you, as she tried to speak.

The ambulance stopped and parked behind the hospital, Cecile gasped, and her hand fell from Blaine's. A paramedic placed his stethoscope on her heart, shook his head, and said, "I'm sorry, sir, she's gone, her heart just stopped."

Blaine choked and sobbed, "Come back! Cecile, come back."

Walking beside Blaine, as they removed Cecile from the ambulance, Farron motioned for an intern, "I think you should give my father a sedative; if you don't quiet him, he may go too. My father is not young, and I don't know how strong his heart is."

A half-hour later, both Blaine and Cecile lay on stretchers next to each other in a receiving room; Doctor McFinney entered, examined Cecile, sighed, and covered her face.

Turning to Blaine, and speaking softly," he said, "I wish we could have saved her; Cecile had a long hard fight with her asthma. I know it's difficult to accept, but if it helps, know that she will suffer no more. McFinney placed his stethoscope on Blaine's chest and listened. "I'm going to keep you here for a few days. We do not want to lose you too. I'll have you put in a little room upstairs, and Farron can stay with you."

Blaine reached for Farron's hands, "Without Cecile, I have

no reason to live."

Farron gripped his father's hand, "Mother would not want to hear you say that, dad. If she had her way, she would be here with you, but the Lord decided her suffering should end, and now she is at rest with God. You have a reason to live; you have us, and we need you. You also have a grandson who will need you as he grows into a man. If the Lord thought you should be with mother, you would be. But, God knows you have a purpose here on earth with us."

Mass held at St. Patrick's Catholic Cathedral found the church filled with Cecile's friends who viewed her remains, said a prayer and walked on. The cemetery next to the church with space awaiting saw Cecile's casket lowered into the ground. Blaine fell to his knees, sobbing, and dropped a handful of soil in after her. Everyone left, except the family, and Blaine remained crying until a hand touched his shoulder, "You must come now," Juliette said, "people are waiting for you at the house. I know you don't want to leave her, but you must. It was the same for me, but you see, I did not pass with my beloved; I am here. All your friends who loved Cecile are waiting to express their condolences."

Blaine put his hand on Juliette's and rose to his feet. "You tried to save her; I am forever thankful," he said and slowly walked beside her, "I know she is with God."

Chapter 12

When Juliette left France, she did not expect to fall in love with America, and yet, here she was in the kitchen cooking for guests in a house that had become her home. Now, she was in love with more than the country; she was in love with Blaine and did not try to conceal her feelings. But Blaine, grieving over the loss of Cecile, failed to notice and each day left the house with Farron, sat on the bow of Farron's boat, breathed the sea air, and felt close to his lost love with memories taking him back to the happiness they shared. It was on one such day that Farron left the helm, let the boat drift, joined his father, and allowed his passengers to watch their lines without his assistance. "Dad," he said, "I know how you miss mom, but you must begin to live again; mother died over a year ago, and you need joy in your life. Have you not noticed how Juliette caters to you?"

"What?" Blaine stared at Farron and shook his head, "What are you saying?"

"I am suggesting that it is time for you to stop living in the past and come to life. A beautiful woman cooks all your meals, waits on you, worries about you, and you do not notice. Juliette is in love with you, dad!"

"Son," Blaine responded, "I can never love again; I will not be unfaithful to your mother."

"Mother is in heaven, dad, and mother would not want you to be alone. If you ever have another woman, mother would be

happy to know it was Juliette, and you need to remember how close they were, almost like sisters."

Blaine shook his head, "Yes, at first, Cecile was jealous of Juliette, but in time she loved her and appreciated the way she took over the kitchen and did things Cecile could no longer do." Silence followed, and then Blaine said, "I guess you're right, son, I need to come alive and stop living in the past."

"Yes, you do, and when we get these fishermen back to port, we will clean the boat, go into Delaney's, have a drink, and go home, clean up and get ready for dinner. Tonight, when Juliette waits on you, please notice the extra attention she gives you."

Blaine laughed, "My son, the matchmaker!"

It was nearly four in the afternoon when Farron unloaded his happy fishermen at the dock. "It was a great day," one said, "how about doing the same thing next week?"

"If the weather allows, you bet!" Farron replied. "If the weather is bad, give me a call, and we will do it another day." All agreed. Farron and Blaine cleaned the boat and headed for the bar where each had a Bloody-Mary. "I love this drink," Blaine said, "but we shouldn't have too many because it will kill our appetites."

That evening as Blaine sat at his private table in the dining room, Juliette entered and sat across from him, "May I join you," she asked? Every night I see you sitting here by yourself, and you

look so lonely. I know you are finding it hard to be without Cecile, and it hurts my heart to see you grieving."

"Has my son been talking to you," Blaine asked? "Today, while we were at sea with his charter people, he gave me a speech about grieving and coming to life."

"No, indeed not; I have not talked to Farron. I have served all our guests and hoped you would accept my company, but if you wish, I will leave."

"No, please stay, Juliette; I welcome your company. I have much for which to thank you; I must apologize for my behavior."

"There is nothing for which you need to apologize, Blaine. I do not expect thanks for helping when needed. When we first met, you found me to be brazen because I said you were handsome, and you politely put me in my place. However, I did not know I had offended. We, French, say what is in our minds and heart. I still feel the same as I did the day we met; you are a handsome man."

Blaine smiled and looked straight into Juliettes eyes, "And you, my dear, are a beautiful woman. I think one night, instead of dining here, when all this group retires, you and I should leave and dine somewhere else. There is a restaurant in Newport Beach, Fogo De Chao; I think you would like it; how does that sound?"

Juliette reached across the table and held Blaine's hand, "I would love it. I think I have heard that name before; perhaps it's

the place where Philip and Belle dined." She smiled with a twinkle in her eyes, "I think Belle is in love with Philip. He is also French, American born and does not speak a word of French, but according to my daughter, he is

French in all ways. It would not surprise me to see them get married."

Blaine folded his napkin and said, "Come on, we are dining out. Mary, Farron, and Belle, can take care of all this when the guests retire."

Juliette ran into the kitchen, gave orders, laughed, and left.

It was a perfect evening; Blaine and Juliette had a table by a window that allowed them a view of the moonlight on the water. "What would my lovely-lady like to have?"

Juliette smiled, "Let me have a drink to start with, and I will look at the menu; it is large and will take a while for me to decide."

"Of course," Blaine motioned for the waiter, "the lady would like a drink." The waiter bowed and looked at Juliette, "I would like champagne, Louis Roederer if you have it." The waiter nodded, she looked at Blaine, and he said, I'll have the same; bring the bottle." The waiter left and returned, opened the champagne, filled their glasses, and placed the bottle in an ice bucket. "Would you like a few Hors d'oeuvres while studying the menu?"

"Yes," Juliette replied, "bring us a few fried spring rolls, and a dip." As the waiter left, she continued to scan the menu. "Oh,

Blaine, I love this place. You can have a steak, lamb chops, pork, and anything you like. I suppose you will want a steak, but I would like rice, with vegetables, Kun Pao Chicken, and Sweet and Sour Pork."

"You are right," Blaine said, "I will have lamb chops, two fresh pear halves filled with mint jelly, asparagus, and mixed vegetables. And, to top it off, more wine, coffee, and a big slice of chocolate topped cream-cheese pie."

Juliette giggled, "I will have coffee and caramel custard."

After dinner, Blaine drove to the beach, parked, and found a bench near the water. A slight breeze blew off the sea, and Juliette shivered. Blaine put his arm around her, "You are cold?"

"A little, but your arm feels gentle and warm. It has been a long time since I have felt a man's arm around me. I know that I appear to be gay and happy, and in ways I am. Still, something is missing. We all need someone to love, someone to fill the empty hours. One can be in a crowd, and be lonely, can't one?"

Blaine turned Juliette's face toward him and kissed her. "We need not be lonely," and she returned his kiss.

A few days later, a message came for Belle, an offer to do a few television appearances, advertisements for different products; she was excited and told Philip about the offer, but his reaction was not good; he grew morose. "I don't want you mixing with the Hollywood crowd."

"Philip! I am an actress; I came here to make films and be

on the screen! I've waited but heard nothing about making another film, and the producers saw me in 'No Time To Lose.' I thought once seen, I would get other offers, but I've had none."

"What difference does it make? I thought you loved me," Philip complained. "I thought we would get married, and you would be content."

"Married? You never asked me to marry you," Belle replied.

"Well, I am asking now, Belle; what's it going to be, me or movies?"

As much as Belle wanted to be a star, she could not give up Philip. With tears in her eyes, Belle put her arms around Philip's neck and said, "You; it is going to be you." Meanwhile, in the back of her devious little mind, Belle thought; we will marry, and he will change his mind and let me make movies. "My love," she said, "when do you want to get married?"

"As soon as possible, tomorrow."

"How is that possible?" Belle laughed. "I am not a citizen of the United States!"

"It doesn't matter. We can go to the County Clerks office and get a marriage license; you will show your passport, and I will show my driver's license, and I will pay a fee. We will go to the County Court House, and an officiant will hear our vows; we will exchange rings, I will kiss you, and we will be legally married." With his arms around Belle, "Je t'aime, tres beaucoup,

 my love," he said. "Does my French make you happy?"

Belle returned his kiss and laughed, "You have been practicing. Oui, Je t'aime; I love you too, Philip, but you are too fast. Your proposal is so sudden and unexpected; my head is spinning. I must tell Juliette, and she must be with us."

"Yes, of course; she will be one of our witnesses," Philip replied, "and my mother will be the other."

Belle held up her hand, "I do not have a ring!"

Philip laughed, "You are a little devil trying to think of things to slow our marriage. Don't you love me, Belle? Rings are not a problem; this afternoon, when I am through work, we can go to the jewelry store, and you can pick out the rings you want. Not many brides can do that."

"If we marry, Philip, will you allow me to do the ads for television?"

Angry, Philip pulled away from Belle and asked, "What if I say no, Belle, will you refuse to marry me?"

"You are angry," Belle returned, "I love you; I cannot refuse to marry you! Nevertheless, I would like to do that job; it pays a lot of money, and only a fool would walk away from it."

Frowning, Philip relented, "Very well, but first, we marry, and after that, you can do the ads. When are you supposed to meet with this Mort guy? I want to meet him too."

"I will call him now," Belle replied, reached for the phone,

and smiled, "this phone brought me you."

It took a while for Belle to reach Mort, and when she did, she found him perturbed. "Where in the hell have you been," he asked? "I've been trying to reach you; I need an answer. Do you want this job, or don't you?"

"I want it, Mort, that's why I'm calling," Belle returned, "but I need a contract or something, don't I? Why don't you meet me the day after tomorrow in front of Delaney's, and we'll have lunch."

"Why the day after tomorrow," Mort asked?

"Because, Mort, tomorrow I am getting married, and my last name will be Dubois."

"Well, I'll be damned," Mort uttered and asked if he knew her intended.

"No, you don't know him, but I told you that he is handsome enough to be a movie star."

Mort laughed, "Wait until I tell Sol! Okay, we will see you the day after tomorrow around noon at Delaney's, and we will toast the bride and groom."

Belle hung up the phone, rushed to Philip, and said, "Now I must tell mama and Blaine while you finish your day's labor." She kissed him, "Try to get off early; we don't want the stores to close."

"I will be here at three, and you be ready."

Belle rushed to tell everyone and invite them to the wedding. Farron looked at Mary, they both laughed, and Mary said, "We would love to join you, but Farron and I will be working in the kitchen; we cannot leave our little toddler, John; but, what a wonderful surprise this is!" She rushed to put her arms around Belle, but Juliette was there, hugging Belle and kissing her. "Mon be-be', je suis si heureux et je serai avec toi pour te donner, Philip."

Juliette looked for Blaine, "Did I tell you? I knew Belle was in love with this American born Frenchman, and they are getting married. We must go with them and witness the marriage."

"Wait, Juliette, you are too quick! Did I hear you say we must witness their marriage?"

Belle kissed Blaine, "Yes, Philip and I are to be web tomorrow at the Courthouse. I would love a church wedding, but Philip wants a quick wedding." She then told them about her television offer and explained that it upset Philip so much he proposed. "We are going this afternoon to buy rings."

"I had no idea that it was so easy to get married," Blaine said, "this is a changing world, isn't it?" He looked at Juliette and winked; courtships seem to be a thing of the past. Today, we fall in love, and tomorrow we get married as if the world is going to end, and we have no time to lose; we must do it now!

Juliette smiled, blushed, and in a quiet tone, remarked, "We must go with these children and hear them make their promises.

I wish it were not so sudden because I feel that marriage vows should be made in church and blessed by the priest; we are Catholic."

Blaine went to Juliette and held her hand, "I agree," he said, "but we will not try to stand in the way of this wedding; perhaps, one day, they may choose to renew their vows in the church."

"Yes, I will talk to Philip about that; he too is Catholic, and I am surprised that he insists upon a quickie marriage, but I am not going to argue!" Belle laughed, "And the day after tomorrow, I meet with Mort and Al to sign an agreement for television ads. Life can be beautiful!"

"Belle," Juliette scolded, "you are still planning to act? What about family? What about children?"

Belle's cheeks turned red, and tears filled her eyes as she remembered another time, with another man, and the loss of him and his child. "S'il te plait maman, ne me le rappelle pas. Laisse moi etre heureux!"

"Pardonne-moi et soyez heureux; je t'aime tres beaucoup."

Understanding, Blaine put his arms around Belle, "You must put away the past. I know how difficult that is. Your mother did not mean to hurt you; she loves you very much, and she wishes you happiness, as do I. Life is not complete without trials, losses, and tears that remain in our hearts forever, but we move on.

And Belle, I and your mother do wish you all the happiness in the world. You and Philip have a long life ahead of you, and although you do not want to think of ever having another child, I think the love between you and Philip will change your mind. Every man wants a son."

Belle kissed Blaine and went to her mother. "Je t'aime maman, je comprendes."

"Wonderful," Blaine declared, "and now I have a surprise for you, Belle, and everyone, "I am in love with Juliette. I did not think I could ever love again because Cecile was my heart, and we lived through so many trials, hurts, and losses over the years. I honestly thought when Cecile died, I could never love again. But then, one day, my observant son told me I should open my eyes and live again. He also said to me that Juliette was in love with me, and he was right. We are in love, but not hasty; we are not young, and perhaps we have no time to lose but feel that we need to know each other better. Juliette had a life before me, as I had before her, and now we must talk about all the years that went before we met. I have not asked her to marry me," Blaine turned to Juliette and reached for her hand, "Beautiful Juliette, will you marry me?"

Everyone except Blaine and Farron began to cry, and Juliette went to Blaine, put her arms around his neck, kissed him, and said, "I thought you would never ask."

Chapter 13

Blaine and Juliette witnessed Belle and Philip's wedding, after which Philip asked, "Do you mind if I take my bride home? I know a celebration usually follows a wedding, but Belle has not met my mother and has not seen where we live. I would like to take her there now, and then return to the boarding house for drinks and to celebrate with everyone."

Juliette kissed Belle, "I can see by the expression on your face that you are anxious to know where you are going to live. I wish your mother-in-law had been with us, but I suppose she had a good reason for not coming.

"My mother is like a butterfly flitting from flower to flower," Philip returned, "but once you know her, you will love her. We will see you for dinner." He opened the car door, "Come with me, wife; you have a surprise ahead." Without taking his eyes off of the road, he continued to explain. "You know nothing about the Newport Beach area where Farron docks his boat to pick up his charters. My mother and I live on Lido Isle, a small man-made island located in Newport Harbor; it is solely residential with no commercial facilities. The island's Club House hosts community parties, and we have a Yacht Club and a small snack bar. Lido Isle has only one link to the city, a small bridge. My mother has a quaint little Cape Cod-style single-story home near the shore."

"Stop!" Belle screamed, "We are not going to live with your mother, are we?"

"Yes," Philip answered, "and you will love the house, my mother, and Lido Isle. I see it as an artist colony. He crossed a bridge, drove down a narrow street, and parked in front of a charming cottage. A casually dressed woman came out to greet them, smiled, and kissed Philip. "Do forgive me, dear, for not coming to your wedding; I had guests. She turned to Belle, and you are Philip's beautiful bride."

Belle's mouth opened and closed as she searched for words, "You look familiar, have we met?"

Philip began to laugh, "Irene, my mother, is an actress; she is not a star but is in many films."

Irene smiled, "Yes, I am what they call an extra, and on occasion, I get a part that allows me a line or two. Philip hates it when I have a role; he does not like Hollywood, but I love it! A couple of stars own little getaway places here, and I run into one or two of them now and then." Irene opened the door and said, "Welcome to my humble abode. I hope you will be happy here. You will not see much of me as we have separate halves to the house. The front half is mine," and of course, we share the living room and the fireplace, when needed. She kept walking toward the back, "and this is yours and Philip's half of the house. It is not French but has a lovely garden that opens onto the beach. The air is fresh, and the birds will wake you in the morning, seagulls. As fishing crafts leave the harbor, the seagulls follow, making a terrible squawking noise."

Belle put her arms around Irene, "You are a sweetheart,

thank you for making me feel welcomed. I think we can be good friends. Since leaving Paris, I've met many people and lived a life much different from life in France."

"And how did you come to leave France," Irene asked?

Belle glanced at Philip, "Oh, I thought Philip might have told you. I left France to star in a movie in Alaska. We will talk about it one day. And, I must say, this son of yours failed to tell me his mother is an actress!"

"That's because he does not think of me as an actress; I am his mom. You can imagine how surprised I was when he told me he was in love with an actress, and now I am doubly surprised as he failed to tell me you were a star."

Belle laughed, "A star? That remains to be seen. We have not yet seen the movie, but are promised a viewing. You might know the producer, Mort Levy."

Irene mulled the name around in her mind, "No, I don't think I do, but then, I am terrible with names, and remember, I am only an extra who does walk-ons, and an occasional bit part; hardly noticeable."

"But Irene," Belle allowed, "isn't this fantastic, you and I are in the same business, I married your son, Philip, and he is an American born Frenchman?"

"Yes, Philip was born in Louisiana, and we moved west when he was very young. His father met me in New Orleans; I was acting in a play in Le Petit Theatre. We met, fell in love, married, moved west, and Edward, his father, got a job at one of the studios, painting scenery. He died at an early age from lung cancer, caused, of course, from painting." Irene pointed to a large comfortable chair, "Please, why are we standing? I know I'm babbling because I am excited. Make yourself comfortable, and I will bring tea and," she giggled, "crumpets." She left the room, and Philip, with an amused expression on his face, said, "Well?"

"I feel like I am dreaming, Philip. From the moment we met, life has moved too fast. I love you, I adore your mother, and I love this place. Is it real? Are we married, and are we here? Blaine was right; we didn't take the time to get acquainted, I know nothing about you."

"We know all we need to know," Philip answered. "We love each other, and you are my wife to have and to hold until death, us do part."

"Don't say that word, Philip. Don't ever say that death will part us."

Irene returned, "Perhaps we should have wine instead of tea, but the problem is, I don't have any wine!" She held a cup up and said, "Heres to my two children, may your love last forever, and may you have many children."

Philip laughed, "You sound like, Blaine."

"And who is Blaine," Irene asked?

Belle replied, "I live in a boarding house between Long

Beach and here. As fate would have it, Farron, Blaine's son, was my costar in the movie we made in Alaska. It's a long story. When I came to the United States, Mort, our producer, had not arranged a place for me to live, and Farron offered me an apartment in the building owned by his father, Blaine. They have all been so kind. I brought my mother to America, and now, she too lives with Farron's family in the boarding house."

"Yes," Philip interrupted, "now we must go, dine with them and get Belle's things. Would you like to join us mother? It will be a celebration, and you can meet Belle's mother."

"Not yet, dear; you are like your father, too quick. I will meet them another time. I have friends to dine with at the Club House tonight." Irene kissed Belle on the cheek, "You must bring your mother; I wish to meet her."

Philip reached for the phone and called Farron, "We are on our way," he hung up, kissed Irene, took Belle by the hand, and said, "come on, wife, we have a date."

The dining room, filled with all the houseguests, cheered as they entered, and all the men kissed the bride. Juliette threw her arms around Philip and then turned to Belle, "Now you make this wonderful, handsome, man, a good wife. Be faithful and do not test him."

"I will be a good wife and try not to anger him, mother."

"Now, tell me," Juliette asked, "where are you living?"

"Oh, mother," Belle replied, "we are living in a beautiful

 home on a little island in Newport Beach, with Philip's mother."

"No, you cannot live with his mother," Juliette exclaimed! "Your marriage will not last; his mother will interfere with your life!"

"No, she will not, mother," Belle argued, "Irene, Philip's mother is wonderful, and she is an actress, so we have a lot in common."

Juliette narrowed her eyes, "You are a dreamer."

"Ma-Mere', look around you, and what do you see? You see happiness, Farron and Mary live with Farron's father, and Cecile, when she was alive, and always happy. If it worked for them, it could work for Philip and I." Belle looked around the room and saw that Mary was going from table to table talking with the guests,

"Am I imagining," Belle asked, "or is Mary looking a little round in the belly?"

"You are not imagining, Belle; Mary is pregnant, and Farron is thrilled. He is praying for a daughter, but Mary is growing so fast, he might end up with twins." Seeing how hard Mary works, Farron hired a very nice Mexican lady to help in the kitchen. Her name is Maria, and she is an excellent cook; the menu has changed a lot. Some of the guests complained, but after the first week, they were happy. Tonight we have a Fiesta for you and Philip. On the menu is Pork Carnitas with a salsa, Guacamole, Pickled red cabbage, warmed tortillas, homemade tortilla chips, chopped white onions, coriander, cilantro leaves, lime wedges,

marinated chicken, chicken fajitas, shredded chicken, beef fajitas, Mexican shredded beef, fish tacos, cheese dip, Mexican corn salad, Avocado corn salad, Mexican grilled corn with chipotle adobo sauce, Mexican red rice, refried beans shredded cheeses, avocado slices hot dressings and mild sauces and churros. It is all on a large table in the middle of the dining room, and everyone takes their plates and fills them with what they want, and for those who want a drink, we have coffee, tea, milk, and Margaritas."

Belle took Philip's hand and said, "Oh, Philip, I wish your mother would have come."

Philip smiled, "I don't think she would have enjoyed it."

Juliette heard and walked away.

A slap on the back and Philip turned to see who it was, "Philip," Farron said, "I have a charter tomorrow, and since you live so close to the Newport Beach Harbor, would you like to go along. You can catch some bass and take them to your mother to cook for dinner."

Philip laughed out loud, "I don't know how to fish, and if I did and caught fish, my mother would not have them in the house. My mother is a very spoiled woman; she is an actress and only eats when waited on. When I was a boy and dad was alive, things were a little different because dad liked to cook, and he did. Mother gave me breakfast, cereal, and that was it."

With lifted eyebrows, Juliette looked at Belle and sent her

an all-knowing look. Belle tried not to notice, but Juliette came to her and said, "Good luck, dear. You might want to move back into the boarding house."

"Ne fais pas avec moi la malchance, mama. J'aime Philip et L'amour vainc tout."

"Nous prions," Juliette returned.

"Here now, Belle, what is all this," Philip asked? Are you two arguing? We are here to celebrate and be happy!"

"I am happy, Philip, but I think my mother is jealous because we are living with your mother. Take me home; it was a mistake to come here."

"No, Belle, we cannot leave. This celebration is for us, and they have gone to a lot of trouble and expense. We are here, and here we stay."

Bell shrugged, and in the back of her mind thought Philip is commanding; that will change, or we will part. I love him, but he is in for a surprise; he is not the only man alive, and I can never love him the way I did Bill.

Mary came to Belle, kissed her, and said, "Look at this. I am getting fat, no?"

Belle returned, "Oui! And you are happy."

"Yes," Mary returned, "and now that you are married, I expect that soon, you will be the same. A home is not a home without children."

Belle laughed, "No. Philip has not said he wants children." She smiled devilishly, "I will surprise him one day, but it will be difficult to bring up a child while working. I accepted a television offer and have done a couple of funny advertisements for toothpaste and kitchen cleansers. I had no idea there was so much money to be made doing television ads; it's fun, and I am at home working with makeup artists, directors, and other actors."

Mary glanced across the room and saw that Juliette was watching and listening, and with a drink in hand, she came to them, tilted her head, and asked, "Belle, darling, did you not say that Philip's mother is an actress?"

"Yes, she is, but not a star; she is a bit player."

"I see," Juliette replied, "she is an actress, and she has a son; I wonder how she managed?"

"Tu es mechante Maman! Pourquoi? Es tu jaloux?"

"Pace que je suis inquiet."

Blaine interrupted, "You must speak English; our guests are confused and are wondering what is happening."

Juliette smiled, "Of course, we are impolite; this is a family matter and should not be discussed at this gala affair. My daughter and her husband should mingle with their guests and enjoy themselves." She looked at Belle, "I think you know everyone here, and you should introduce your new husband to all." Smiling, she asked, "Philip, would you care to meet those you don't already know?"

"You are a sweetheart, Juliette; yes, please introduce me, and while I am getting to know everyone, Belle can drift around and talk with all her friends."

As they walked away, Belle glared at both, and Blaine touched her arm. "Let me get you a drink; a margarita will make you feel much better." He took her to the bar, "This is not much like it was while you lived here. Your mother, along with Mary, now runs the place. Juliette is a marvel, and she was so good to Cecile; how can I ever repay her?"

Belle eyed him, thoughtfully, "You are in love with my mother, N'est-ce pas?"

"Obvious, isn't it?" Blaine returned.

"Oui, and I am happy because she needs someone, and you are a good man."

Juliette neared and reminded Belle to move around and talk with the guests, "They are all your friends, and have often asked about you. Philip is having a good time and is enjoying the guests, the food, and the margaritas."

" But mother, they are all such peasants."

Shocked, Blaine spoke up. "Belle, I am surprised and disappointed in you. When did you become such a snob? Your husband, a peasant, works for the telephone company, and probably installed and connected most of their phones. I think you have forgotten how you met! As I recall, he installed your phone, and it was love at first sight."

Belle looked at Juliette for support and received none. "You are right, Blaine; I am prone to saying the wrong thing. No matter what, nothing can ruin this night because I am married and working on television. My life is complete. I have missed the company of actors."

Juliette took Blaine by the hand, "Come, we should join the others, and Belle, you should join your husband."

Belle smiled, went to the table where Philip was filling his glass, again, and handed him her glass to fill. "I will have a few drinks with you and the guests, dear, and then I think we should thank everyone, excuse ourselves, and leave."

"It's a little early, but I suppose you are right, I have to work in the morning."

An hour later, they crossed the bridge to Lido Isle and found the house dark except for the porch light. "It looks as if your mother has retired; we will sneak in and go to bed."

Philip chuckled, "I thought we might sit out by the water for a while; there is a cool breeze, and this is a night for romance."

Belle giggled and held Philip's hand as they walked down to the water's edge. Kicking off her shoes, she dug her feet into the sand, sat down, and pulled him down to her. "Hold me, and make love to me." He pushed her back in the sand and lay on top of her. "You are a little devil, a teaser, and you drive me wild."

Belle's lips pressed hard against his, and she whispered, "Would you like to have a family?"

"Yes, but I," Belle stopped him, "Then, you will be happy to know that I am expecting."

"What?" Philip sat up, "What the hell are you talking about?"

"I said, I am with child. I knew before we married, but I didn't want to tell you and make you feel you had to marry me."

Tears filled Philip's eyes; he shook his head and tried to fathom her words, had he misunderstood? Trying to control his feelings, he pulled Belle up, held her close, and asked, "Are you sure?"

"Yes, my love, I am sure."

"Slip out of your dress, and I will get out of my clothes," he said, "we drank too many margaritas at the party, and I think we should take a swim and cool off."

Giggling, Belle pulled off her dress, helped Philip disrobe, and rubbed her nude body against his. "You are so handsome, my husband; I love you."

Philip ran his hands down her arms, took her by the hand and walked her into the water, kissed her, and speaking softly, asked, "Isn't this soothing? Let's get farther out and let the water completely cover our bodies."

With her hands on his shoulders, Belle said, "I think this is too deep, Philip, the water feels grand, but I am not a good swimmer."

He held her face in his hands and kissed her, "You are beautiful, and I love you, and you are going to have a baby."

"I am Philip, and I pray it makes you happy."

"Well, my lovely bride, it does not make me happy because the baby is not mine; I am sterile. I cannot produce a child!"

"That can not be true!" Belle cried, "There is a mistake; maybe you were sterile, and it reversed, or they read the wrong person's tests!"

He sobbed, "No mistake, Belle; I did not make your baby! How could you do this to me? I knew you had others, but I thought when we married, it was all behind you; now I learn it was not; you deceived me, lied, and cheated. You are nothing but a cheap little strumpet who gives herself to any man who desires her. How could I be such a fool? I believed you loved me." His fingers bit into her skin, and frightened, she tried to pull away, while he continued to debase her. "If I were a saintly man, I would forgive you, accept your child, and bring it up as if it were mine, but

I am not a saint. You have destroyed my love for you. You are filth, garbage; women like you don't deserve to live." One strong hand held her, and the other went to the top of her head as he pushed her under the water. She struggled, tried to swim, but he held her down until she could fight no more. Without looking back, he slowly left the water, picked up his wet clothing, walked into the house, fell across the bed, wept, and slept until his crazed mind cleared enough for him to know what he must do.

In the morning, he would leave the house quietly while his mother slept. Around eleven, she would rise, make coffee, and call to wake Belle, and when Belle did not join her for coffee, Irene would go looking, find Belle was not there, and contact him. He would chuckle, tell Irene they drank too much at the celebration, came home early, and argued because Belle did not want to leave the party; furious with him, she walked out of the house and said she was going back to celebrate and have some fun. He would then suggest that Irene call Juliette.

As planned, Irene called, and he told her his contrived story. Dismayed, Irene called Juliette.

Juliette answered the phone, "Why no, Irene, Belle is not here. What makes you think she would be? Please don't tell me that our young lovers argued!"

"Yes," Irene replied, "they did. Philip did not tell me what it was about; he simply said I should call and see if Belle were with you. Please, try to reach him and see what he has to say about the fuss that caused her to leave the house?"

Juliette reached Philip late in the afternoon, and when he heard her voice, he said, "Thank God, is Belle with you?"

"No, Philip, Belle is not with us and has not called. What kind of argument brought on enough anger to drive her out of the house and not return?"

"A man," Philip returned, "she is doing commercials and is involved with one of her coworkers. Last night with all the drinks we had, Belle was sarcastic, wanted to fight, and tried to find things with which to hurt me. I made the mistake of laughing, thinking it would calm her, but it angered her, and she spat at me; said she was pregnant, but not by me. Laughing, she said it over and over and wouldn't stop. Not knowing what else to do, I slapped her face and shook her to bring her out of it. She broke away from me and ran from the house. I don't know where she went! I am like a crazy person, trying to work while fearing she might do something drastic! Now, what can I do? Belle is not with you and has not called me. What should I do?"

Juliette cried, "I don't believe Belle has been unfaithful, Philip; she loves you. When, where, how could she have an affair with someone else?"

"I told you; while doing the ads for television. She is beautiful and desirable; every man wants her. She is your daughter, and you know her weakness; she is gullible, loves attention, and gives too easily. Juliette, your daughter, loved one man, and he died when the ship went down in Alaska; she will never love another. Belle does not love me."

I know Belle is stubborn and self-willed, but she will come back to you. She does love you, Philip."

Chapter 14

Three days later, Paul Steller, a Hollywood writer, strolled down to his dock to check on his skiff and found something he was not looking for; the sun shined down on Belle's body, bumping against his skiff. He first thought to pull Belle up and out of the water, then realized he should not touch her and called Harbor Patrol. Minutes later, several boats arrived, the police, and an ambulance parked in his driveway. Questions followed all of which he could not answer, as he did not know the victim.

Neighbors crowded around to watch as they took Belle away. "I think I know who that woman is," a man said, "I don't know her name, but she might be the bride of Philip Dubois. His mother lives in a cottage a couple of doors down the street; she's an actress. Follow me, and I'll show you which house is hers."

Three officers and the informant went to Irene's door, and one knocked. Irene answered, disheveled, and half asleep. Surprised to see officers, she asked, "My word, isn't it a bit early to be knocking on doors? What can I do for you?"

They explained, and one held his cell phone in front of her, "Do you know this person?"

Shocked, Irene backed away, "Why yes, that's my daughter-in-law," and looking as if she might faint, she asked, "how can this be?" She called for Philip, "Philip, wake up and come here. There are a couple of officers at the door."

Looking tired, Philip came to the door, and when he saw the officers, he said, "Sorry, I'm not awake. I haven't slept well since my wife, Belle, stormed out of the house a few nights ago; she's very headstrong; I went looking for her but couldn't find her.   Now here you are, and I have to ask, what has Belle done? Is she in jail? She was pretty drunk and angry when she left."

The officers showed him the picture of Belle, "I think you had better dress and come with us. We need to ask you a few questions, and you need to identify the body."

Philip looked as if he were going to pass out, "My God, my God," he uttered and turned, "Give me a minute."

"Sir, we will stop at the city morgue; you can look at the body and identify your wife; following that, we will take you in for a few questions."

Philip looked at Belle's body, "My beautiful wife," he sobbed, "What have you done?"

"Then, this is your wife?" the officer with him questioned.

"Yes, this is my beautiful Belle," Philip returned. "Her mother should be told."

"Her mother knows," the officer replied, "she came to us, reported her daughter missing, saw the photo, and says you killed her daughter. Of course, we can't accept that."

Juliette and Blaine were waiting at the precinct as officers led Philip through the room. Juliette rose from her chair and

shouted, "That's him! Murderer!"

Blaine subdued her and made her sit. "We don't know how it happened, Juliette, and if you are not quiet, they will make us leave."

Accompanied by the two arresting officers, Philip entered a small windowless room for questioning. One officer offered him coffee and said, "We don't enjoy doing this, but we must ask you a few questions."

Philip started to reply but thought better of it. "I'm sorry, but before you bombard me with questions about which I know nothing, I would like to see my lawyer."

"If you have committed no crime, there is no need for an attorney," one officer warned.

Philip, knowing his rights, repeated, "I will say nothing without my lawyer."

"If you have not committed a crime, why do you insist on having a lawyer. Your wife is dead, drowned, and you know nothing about it?"

Philip shook his head and did not reply.

"Your mother tried to place a bond for your release, but we must hold you for further investigation because your mother-in-law says your wife was a good swimmer and questions how she could have drowned. With no evidence of excessive drinking in her system, how did it happen?"

"Are you accusing me of murder?" Philip stood up and pounded the desk, "I demand to see my lawyer." He sat down, folded his arms, and angrily glared at them.

"We will need his name," one answered.

"Talk to my mother; she will give you all the information you need."

One officer left the room and returned, "Melvin Briskin will be here shortly. He is your attorney, is he not?" Philip nodded.

Twenty minutes later, Melvin entered, "I have posted a bond for your release, and we can leave. There is absolutely no evidence pointing to murder; your bride's death was accidental, and until proven otherwise, you cannot be held."

"One last question," one officer said, "did you know your wife was pregnant?"

Philip looked at Briskin, and he nodded, "Yes, I knew, but Belle did not want the baby; she miscarried a boy-child many years ago, and the memory haunted her."

"Then, you are her second husband?"

"No, I am her first; the other pregnancy was from a lover." As the words left his mouth, he thought but didn't say, as was this.

Waiting in the outer room with Juliette and Blaine, Irene tried to dismiss the question in her mind. Was it possible? Did Philip murder his wife? Fearing someone would read her mind, Irene looked away. But Juliette had not missed seeing the color leave Irene's face.

"Will there be a further investigation?" Juliette asked one of the officers. "Belle is my daughter, could swim, and I cannot accept her death as accidental. She was celebrating but not intoxicated when she left the wedding party."

"Of course," he replied, "there will be further investigation. Our police department is very comprehensive; if there are no marks on her body, indicating a struggle, then there is the possibility of suicide. The Coroner will thoroughly examine the victim's body."

Juliette began to cry, "You are talking about my daughter, and I have a right to know everything. Can I see her?"

A conversation followed between the officers and the chief inspector, allowed Juliette and Blaine to view Belle's body.

Juliette looked down at Belle and cried, "So small, so beautiful, and now she's gone. Philip murdered her, Blaine, I know he did. I don't know why, but an inner voice tells me Philip killed her. I know he loved her, and I thought he was gentle and kind, but Belle could be selfish and often caused herself unnecessary problems. My fault, I was not strict. She was such a beautiful child, so easy to give her everything she wanted."

After being released, shaking inwardly, Philip strove to look like a grieving husband. They knew Belle was pregnant, and soon they would learn the truth about him. What should he do? He must getaway, but how, and where should he go? Mexico was too close; he would head for Canada and say nothing to Irene. Late that night, he got in his car and quietly drove away.

The next morning, finding his car missing, Irene knew her son was guilty of murder, and she knelt, prayed, and cried, "Lord, please forgive my son and keep him safe." The phone rang; Irene thought not to answer but decided she must. It was Juliette, "I would like to speak to Philip, please; I am Belle's mother."

Irene choked out, "Yes, of course, just give me a moment; I'll wake him. He has not slept well since Belle's death, and neither have I." She left the phone, went to a door, and called out for Philip, waited a while, and as if she had been in another room, closed a door, and picked up the phone, "Are you still there?" she asked.

"Yes. Tell Philip I will wait," Juliette answered.

What should she do? Irene called for Philip again, slammed a door, and returned to the phone. "I am so sorry," Irene said, "I went to his room, and no one is there. He works for the telephone company, perhaps there is trouble on the line, and Philip might have gone to help. I haven't watched the news, have you?"

"Oh, never mind," Juliette answered, "I will call back later."

"I'll call you when I hear from Philip. He is so troubled, I fear for him and hope he is doing simple installations. The weather is terrible; I pray he is not climbing telephone poles."

At midnight, feeling safe, Philip raced north on the Pacific Coast Highway; he was free. A week from now, no-one would know where he was. The sound of a horn and Belle's face appeared before him. Was it Possible? Blinded by the oncoming lights, Philip shook his head and blinked his eyes. Something crossed the road in front of him; he shoved down hard on the brakes, and his car careened out of control from side to side, crashed through a railing, rolled, and bounced down a rocky incline, and landed upside down in the water and rocks on the edge of the Pacific Ocean. Attempting to open a window, Philip pounded and pushed on the door, but to no avail, water seeped in above his chin; he screamed and water-filled his mouth, nose, and lungs.

On the hill above the wreckage, Jim, the truck driver, stopped, made his way down the hillside, and waded through the water to the car. He looked in, saw Philip, and picked up a rock, broke the front window, reached through the opening, and struggled to pull Philip out, but too late; Philip was gone.

When Juliette heard of Philip's death, she cried and put her head on Blaine's shoulder. "My beautiful Belle got her revenge; Philip's death was the same as hers; he drowned."

Blaine held her close, "You and I must go away; take a trip. We need to go someplace where you can forget."

"Oh, Blaine, how can I forget? I would love to get away, but I can't; I must stay here and take care of the guests. Mary can't do it; she is getting bigger every day. Seven months, or less, from now, she will have the baby or babies."

"We have Maria, and we can hire another woman to help. Maybe Maria has a relative who needs work."

A voice came from the other side of the room, "Si tengo otras dos; mi hermana y mi hermano."

Juliette laughed, "Blaine, Maria has a brother and sister who can work for us. I think we should try them for a week or two before we run away.

Looking hopeful, Maria continued, "Ellos hacen todo!"

"Blaine," Juliette said, "Let's give it a try. Maria says that they will do everything. And I have taught Maria how to cook the things our guests like; she can also bake. Nevertheless, we must wait and watch them for two weeks, and then we can leave on our trip, to where Blaine?"

"Where would you like to go? How about the Hawaiian Islands?"   Giving it thought, Juliette smiled, "How about Paris? I could show you my country. Paris is so beautiful!"

"I know Paris," Blaine returned, "remember, I was in the service. "I love you, Juliette, but I had in mind the islands, and -and – I thought it would be a nice romantic place to get married."

Juliette took Blaine by the hand and led him into another room, "My dear loving man, you have just proposed to me in the kitchen in front of Maria. Have you told anyone else that you

want to marry me? We must think of Farron, Mary."

Maria stuck her head in, "I will help Farron and Mary, and

so will my sister and brother."

They began to laugh, "There is no privacy in this house!"

Blaine lifted Juliette off of the floor and kissed her. "I love you, my bride to be, and in two weeks, we are off to Maui, the Magic Isle. We will get our State of Hawaii marriage license, get married in Maui, and stay at the Kaanapali Villas."

"And how do you know all this," Juliette asked?

"My sweet, I think I fell in love with you the first day we met, but I didn't know it; Cecile was alive, and I loved Cecile with all my heart. I never thought I could love again, but my dear son told me to wake up and get a life, and now, here we are. I have thought about this for months, and looked into everything." Blaine kissed Juliette again, "This is just what we two need. I feel young! If Mary were not expecting, we could ask her and Farron to join us, but I planned this trip to Maui as our private escape. We've had our share of sadness, and now we must put it behind us and live."

Tears filled Juliette's eyes, "But, Blaine, there are some things I can't forget.

Blaine held her close, "The moving hand writes and having writ moves on, and we cannot move it back to change things. Our lives are in God's hands, and we cannot argue with God. I needed you, and he knew you would need me; the rest is up to us. There is no reason for us to remain here; Farron and Mary are happy; we are not young, and I don't want my wife to be a kitchen maid."

"You are right, Blaine! We are not young, with no time to lose, so let us delay no longer; let's go to Maui and get married."

Six months later, Farron became the father of twin baby boys, and to Mary, he said, "I love you more than life, and now look what you have done!" Mary caressed his face, "Yes, look what we have done; you have a new crew for your ship." Farron laughed, "Not for a few more years, but they will grow and be fishers, like their dad."

www.ingramcontent.com/pod-product-compliance
Lightning Source LLC
Chambersburg PA
CBHW061254120726
48001CB00001B/293